# DARK THREAT

## BY KIMBERLY ROSE JOHNSON

Dark Threat
Published by Sweet Rose Press
U.S.A.

All Scripture quotations, unless otherwise indicated, are taken from the Holy Bible, New International Version®, NIV®. Copyright ©1973, 1978, 1984, 2011 by Biblica, Inc.™ Used by permission of Zondervan. All rights reserved worldwide. www.zondervan.com The "NIV" and "New International Version" are trademarks registered in the United States Patent and Trademark Office by Biblica, Inc.™

ISBN 978-1-954722-00-2

# 1

Trinity Lockhart flashed her press badge. "I'm covering the exhibit for KXB News." Working for the number one news channel in Seattle usually got her into ticketed events, though not always. She held her breath and flashed her best smile.

The stocky man in a tux raised his eyebrow but let her pass.

"Thank you." She ambled farther into the gallery looking for anything suspicious. A business card on the floor caught her eye. Though tempted to step over it, she paused, reached down, and retrieved it. A mystery informant told her the high-end Seattle art gallery fenced stolen art. She didn't want to miss a clue.

Someone bumped into her. She lost her footing. A sandy-blond-haired man grasped her forearm.

"Careful. You shouldn't stop in the middle of a walkway." He grinned, but the smile didn't reach his eyes.

She shivered from his icy demeanor. She wanted to

dismiss him in the same way she wanted to dismiss the business card on the floor, but he could also offer a clue. "Sorry. I didn't mean to block traffic." She offered her hand. "I'm Trinity with KXB News. What drew you to the exhibit this evening?"

He rolled his eyes and brushed past her. Maybe he was one of the traffickers fencing stolen art or even her mystery informant. Though more than likely, he was simply a snooty art connoisseur. Not that she thought all lovers of art were that way, but he definitely fit the stereotype.

Trinity dropped the gallery's business card into her silver clutch. She wandered farther into the high-end Seattle art gallery, noting luxury at every angle. From the luxe leather covered seating strategically placed for viewing the art, to the marble pillars displaying sculptures.

Her black heels clicked on the shiny wood floor. She slipped off her long black coat revealing her one and only little black dress she wore maybe once a year. As a crime beat reporter, she had little use for a fancy dress, but tonight was the exception. Too bad her tipster hadn't told her who the bad guys were.

A bleached blonde with perfectly manicured eyebrows approached her. "Welcome, I'm Alexis McKenna, your hostess for this evening. I heard you're a reporter." A fake smile revealed perfect white teeth. "However, no one contacted me about covering our exhibit."

"I apologize for the surprise. It was a last-minute decision to feature the exhibit. Would you be available this evening to answer a few questions?" There was something off with this woman. Shouldn't she be gushing that any press showed up to cover her event?

Alexis looked around the gallery. "Where's your camera person?"

"I'm solo tonight." She smiled apologetically. "Last minute."

"Right. Well, I have a couple minutes to spare, but then I must mingle. Mr. Wren's exhibit is our biggest event of the year."

Trinity glanced around the room where servers stood with trays of champagne and hors d'oeuvres. "What can you tell me about the exhibit?"

"All of the pieces pay homage to the Pacific Northwest. His seaside and rainforest pieces are featured this evening."

Trinity nodded. She'd noticed the photography on the wall nearest to them. A dark and moody photo of the churning sea sent foreboding through her. She dragged her gaze from the piece. "Mr. Wren is quite a talent. How did he come to be your featured artist?"

Alexis looked past her distractedly.

Trinity followed her gaze and noted two men entering an employee only area.

The gallery owner, or at least Trinity presumed she was the owner, even though she'd called herself the hostess, directed her attention back to Trinity. "I'm

3

sorry, but I must excuse myself. There's a brochure about Mr. Wren. You're welcome to take one. I'm sure it will answer all your questions." She headed toward the employee only door without waiting for Trinity's response.

Okay, that was weird. Apparently, she didn't appreciate free publicity. Trinity looked around and spotted the brochure. She'd take one then pitch the story to her boss, who had no idea she was here. The anonymous tip she'd received came in late in the day on Friday and there had been no time to follow protocol since Clancy had already left and didn't work weekends.

She strolled through the gallery and pretended an interest in the stellar photography. She loved anything to do with the ocean or water, which was one of the reasons she had sought employment in Seattle, but her instincts told her she needed to get into that backroom. Those men were up to something. Maybe they were the people the tipster was talking about.

Trinity stopped at the display closest to the employee only room and pretended to admire a photo of the Olympic National Forest. A man beside her exclaimed over it. Trinity nodded, surprised to see the rude man who had given her the creeps.

She stepped away from him while he studied the photo. She slid her arms into her coat. If she was going to do this, she needed her hands as free as possible. She slipped to the door and scooted inside the well-lit backroom and closed the door slowly so no one would hear.

Two male voices grabbed her attention. She slipped off her stilettos so they wouldn't hear her coming and then tucked one into each of her coat pockets. On tiptoes, she crept closer to the men and ducked behind a large box.

"The shipment arrives this week. You know what's at stake."

That looked like the stocky man who had been collecting tickets at the door. No wonder Alexis had been distracted by him coming back here. She needed him at the door to collect tickets. What shipment were they talking about? Maybe it was the stolen art Trinity had received a tip about.

Trinity pulled out her smartphone and opened the camera app. The angle was bad, but she took side view pictures of the men anyway.

"I know," a tall man with bushy eyebrows said. "But it's too hot right now."

Stocky man pulled a gun from his waistband. "You know how this works."

Trinity gasped and dropped her purse.

"Who's there?"

Crouching, Trinity retrieved her clutch and then ran toward the gallery floor door and rushed through it. She quickly slipped on her shoes and took off her coat and then casually wandered toward the same man who'd spoken to her earlier. "Mr. Wren is an amazing photographer," she said.

The man held his hand to his chin studying a close

up of a leaf with water droplets. "I agree."

The men from the backroom raced past them and then circled back and stopped directly behind her. The hair on her neck stood on end. "Where'd she go?" One hissed. Sounded like stocky man's voice.

"Beats me. But I know what she looks like. At least from behind. Short with long dark hair, wearing a black coat, and she was barefooted. I don't see any barefooted women and most of the women here are wearing black dresses."

Trinity's pulse thrummed in her ears. What if they noticed her?

"The boss won't like this," stocky man said.

"Keep quiet. I'll deal with the woman."

She sucked in a sharp breath. Her heart pounded.

"You have to find her first."

A thump sounded.

"Hey! That hurt," stocky man said.

Bushy-eyebrow man must have struck the shorter dude. If they kept this up, they'd draw attention to themselves.

"You two follow me. Now," Alexis hissed.

The sound of heels clopping on the wood floor faded. The trio must have walked away. Trinity turned to confirm. She blew out a breath when no one stood behind her. Now what? The man who had been admiring the leaf had moved on. When had that happened? She shook her head. Normally, she would stay to investigate, but normally, there weren't guns and death threats involved. This situation was nothing like what she'd ever experienced.

If Clancy wanted the story, she would come back with cameraman Rick tomorrow for video. In the meantime, she needed to figure out a plan. She couldn't go to the authorities with what she had. Or could she? The hint of an idea formed. It was risky, but she was never one to shy away from a little danger. Even if said danger came in the form of a handsome FBI agent.

# 2

FBI Special Agent Kyle Richards flicked on the kitchen light of his Seattle home as he entered from the garage. A shadow in his living room moved. He pulled his sidearm.

"Don't shoot. It's Trinity Lockhart. I'm a reporter with KXB News." The female crime-beat reporter stood and faced him with arms raised.

"I know who you are." The pint-sized reporter had been a thorn in his side since he'd moved to Seattle a couple of years ago. "How did you know where I live?"

"Your driver's license."

"Come again?"

"I noted your address on your driver's license when you pulled out your wallet to give your buddy money for your lunch that day I stopped you to ask you a question."

He remembered the incident well. He'd been in a rush to grab a late lunch then get to court to testify. He'd been in a hurry and had given Charlie, his buddy and fellow agent, money to pick up his lunch at the food truck they frequented. "Give me one good reason I shouldn't shoot you? You broke into my house." Irritation surged through him though he wouldn't shoot her. He only wanted to scare her so she wouldn't do something this stupid again.

"For starters, I'm not armed. As far as breaking in, it couldn't be helped. I couldn't risk being spotted knocking at your door by anyone who might recognize me. If my presence here got back to my informant, I don't know what would happen."

He eased his Glock into the holster beneath his jacket. He wasn't a fan of the reporter. She had a habit of butting in where she wasn't wanted and causing trouble for those in law enforcement. But he did respect her tenacity. Looking at the brunette, no one would suspect the powerhouse that hid beneath the black blazer. He'd spotted her more than once, pumping iron at the same gym he frequented. "Informant? Why are you here?"

Uncertainty rested on her face. "I need your help."

"Breaking into my home is not a great start."

She waved a hand dismissively. "Once you hear what I have to say, I think you'll say I did the right thing."

"Doubtful." He leaned against the kitchen island facing his open concept living room. "I'm listening."

She motioned to the couch. "May we sit?"

He reached for the switch that would turn on the

living room lights.

"No. Don't."

Concern shot through him. Was Trinity really in trouble? He sat on the couch facing her. "What's this about?"

"As you know, I work the crime-beat."

He knew too well. He nodded.

"Friday evening, I received a tip about Kendall Victoria Gallery in Seattle. The tip alleged that the gallery fences stolen art. They had a private exhibit last night that I attended."

"Uninvited, I presume."

A pout puckered her lips. "Everything appeared to be on the up-and-up at first, but then I noticed the hostess of the show look rather concerned about two men who went into an employees' only area. After a bit, I snuck into the room and heard the men talking."

His shoulders tensed. "Of course you did."

"One was the door monitor who collected tickets for the show. The other guy I didn't recognize."

"What happened?"

"I got as close as I could and took pictures with my phone. One man said things were too hot, and the next thing I knew, the other man pulled out a gun. I gasped and dropped my purse. They heard me. I tore out of there."

A sinking feeling filled him. "Did they see you?"

"Only from behind. I overheard them talking about me."

"How? I thought you left."

"I couldn't run out of the gallery and make a scene. I blended in. They stopped behind me and started talking."

He rubbed his neck, frustration with this woman mounting. "Did you go to the police?"

"No."

"Why not?"

"I don't trust them."

He blew out a breath. "What am I missing here?"

"It's a long story."

He stood. "In that case, let's have dinner while we talk. I haven't eaten all day, and I'm starving." He walked to the kitchen without waiting to see if she followed. He pulled out two frozen meals from the freezer. *Lord, if this is something You want me to get involved in, please let me know.* His compassion for people in general made him want to help, but knowing she was a troublemaker made him want to run the opposite direction.

"What can I do to help?" The uncertainty in her voice surprised him. Trinity always came across as confident and assured.

He turned, holding the boxes. "I have lasagna or a tamale meal."

She tucked a long strand of silky, dark hair behind her ear. Her green eyes widened. "I ate, but thanks." She licked full lips.

He shook his head both at her comment and the

distraction she could become for any man who didn't know how much trouble she caused. He knew too much to ever be that man. "Your loss. These things are great. Though not filling enough." He opened both boxes and then sliced a slit in the top of the lasagna and placed it in the microwave. He'd start with Italian and end with Mexican.

"You were going to share half your meal with *me*?"

He chuckled. "Wouldn't want you to starve. Remember, I'm one of the good guys." He pulled two glasses from the cupboard. "Water?"

"Thanks."

He filled their glasses from the spigot on the fridge and handed it to her. "Now spill." He motioned toward a stool at the island.

"Thanks for not kicking me out."

"Don't thank me yet. What's your story?"

She sat at a barstool and took a long drink. "My dad is a thief. I grew up watching him break into homes for a living."

Of course she had. He almost winced at the first thought, justified or not, that came to his mind once again where Trinity was concerned. He would make a point to look into her dad. "Seems he taught you at least one tool of the trade."

"For an FBI agent, you have a lousy lock on your door."

The microwave beeped. The scent of lasagna made his stomach rumble. He removed part one of his meal and then placed the tamale dinner inside and started it. "It's a deadbolt."

"Not on the back."

He glanced toward the back door and grimaced. He really needed to have a deadbolt installed on that door, but life had been busy. She was definitely a troublemaker, but she could have been a lot worse considering her upbringing. "So you learned how to break into homes from your dad. How does that translate into not trusting the police?"

"I have my dad to thank for that too."

"But you're a crime reporter."

"My way of recompense?" She shrugged. "I didn't approve of my dad's career choice and wanted to do something to make a difference. Use the skills he taught me for good." A dry laugh escaped her lips. "I even tried to join the FBI."

Now there was a shocker, considering how she often made life difficult for his colleagues. "What happened?"

"They didn't want me because of my family history. I moved on to plan B."

"A television reporter? How did you go from not trusting cops to wanting to be in the FBI and then a reporter?"

"Dad didn't have any run-ins with the FBI." She shrugged. "I can't help how I feel about cops. It's ingrained in me."

Which explained her hostility toward police officers

in her reporting. She tried to hide it, but he saw through her. "How did you end up as a crime reporter?"

"That was an accident. I applied to be an investigative reporter, but they had someone in mind already. They liked me and created a spot."

She was likeable. And she was good at her job. Which made her trouble and brought them to their current situation. "So why are you here?"

"My source warned me against contacting the cops or the feds, and honestly, even though I don't have any hang-ups with the FBI in general, I felt inclined to listen."

"Yet here you are in the home of an FBI agent." He understood why she was told not to go to the cops, but why would she be warned against talking to the FBI? Was someone at the agency part of what was going on, or did her informant want to implicate her and knew if she went to the authorities, it would be more difficult? "You sure you can trust your informant?"

"No, but he was right about something going on at the gallery. I came to you because I've seen you in action enough to know you follow the rules."

He did tend to stay inside the lines of the law. "What do you think I can do for you?" He'd always tolerated Trinity. Some might even accuse him of being too polite to her, but it wasn't like they were friends. "Last time I saw you, I had to confiscate some of your footage or risk putting a witness's life in danger."

"That's why I trust you."

Ironic. "I appreciate your confidence in me, but this sounds like a job for the police."

She huffed. "Why? Don't tell me you never look into a tip you get outside the confines of your office. You never investigate without making it official?"

"I didn't say that." He always followed up on tips, but this one seemed more for the local police. He knew the gallery she was referring to—had read online about the exhibit for a local artist last night that was invitation only. The press release stated the gallery had an excellent reputation in the art community and was a highly sought-after venue for local artists. If they were doing what Trinity's source said, then they needed to be stopped.

She raised a brow. "Then help me. I know you're a by-the-book kind of man, but that's why I came to you." Her eyes pleaded with him to help.

He looked away then back at her. "What kind of art are we talking about? Antiquities?" If, and that was a big if, antiquities were being moved through the gallery, the FBI would be interested.

"I don't know. I'm not an art person. I saw glasswork and pottery on display as well as photos and paintings. The featured artist was a photographer. He had a number of ocean photos that were beautiful, but I love anything to do with the ocean." She shrugged.

Her love of the ocean fit the strong pull she had on his resolve. The draw of the ocean tugged on him as well. If he wasn't careful, she could wash him out to sea.

He still had some big questions. "Of all the reporters in Seattle, why did this anonymous source come to you? Could it have anything to do with you in a personal way?"

"I'm the crime-beat reporter for the top news station in the city. Why not come to me?"

He looked past her toward the closed window blinds facing the cul-de-sac he lived on. It wouldn't hurt to check out the gallery, though he suspected the FBI wouldn't want to get involved based on the claims of a reporter known for firing before she aimed. Even if she had the instincts to hit her target every time. "I'll look into it. But don't get your hopes up."

She pulled a business card from her wallet. "Their hours are listed on the back."

He tucked it into his pocket and then ate the lasagna before moving to the tamale meal.

Trinity stood and walked toward the window. She peaked through the blind slats. Her back straightened. "Is it normal for someone to be watching your house?"

"No." His shoulders tensed. He strode over to the window and peered out. A black sedan sat across the street with someone inside. It looked as if Trinity had stepped into more trouble than he realized. "Be right back."

He went out to his garage and pulled night vision binoculars from the glove box. He'd invested in them years ago. He would have said no to helping her, but then he'd be sending her out alone to face whatever it was waiting for her across the street.

He slunk out the side door, crouched beside the house out of sight of the mystery person, and put the binoculars to his eyes. Too bad he'd left his phone inside and couldn't take a picture. He memorized the stranger's face and then headed inside.

Trinity stood near the window with her arms wrapped around her scant middle. "Well?"

"It's a man. Pointy nose, bushy brows, receding hairline."

"The bushy-eyebrow man from the gallery!" Her brow furrowed. "What do I do?" she mumbled as she walked in a small circle. "There must be surveillance cameras at the gallery. That has to be how they tracked me." She stopped and looked at him with wide eyes. "They know I was the one spying on them. I'm sure of it."

He grabbed his phone from the kitchen counter.

"Who are you calling?" Panic filled Trinity's voice.

"The cops. They'll check him out for us."

"Can't you check him out?"

"I could, but it's better this way."

She shook her head. "No. No cops."

Was she serious? One look at the fear in her eyes said yes. "You're killing me. How do you expect to catch this guy without the assistance of the authorities?"

She shrugged.

He sighed and instead of 9-1-1 pressed in Frank Graham's number. He'd have preferred to call his buddy, Marc, but his friend was on an overdue honeymoon and wouldn't return home for another day. Frank was no longer a police officer, but he didn't live far from here, and the man owed him.

"Hey, Kyle. Long time no speak. What's up?"

"You at home?"

"I am."

"I need a favor." He quickly gave him the necessary information and then disconnected the call. Frank was a good man, and he trusted him, which said a lot, even if Frank did leave law enforcement to open a bodyguard business.

"Well?" Trinity looked at him eagerly.

"He should be here in under ten minutes. We'll hang tight and see what he learns. It might be completely unrelated to you."

"I didn't think of that. He sure sounds like the man I saw. What if the man leaves before your friend gets here?"

"That won't happen if he's waiting for you. Have a seat and try to relax." Her wringing hands and jittery motions made him edgy. He needed to remain calm and focused.

She sat and bounced her leg up and down.

"Did you see anyone follow you here?" The man was more than likely waiting for Trinity to leave so he could follow her home.

"I wasn't paying a lot of attention." She bit her bottom lip and shook her head slightly. "I know better than that. My dad taught me to watch my back. Be aware of my surroundings. Always pay attention to what was going on around me."

"You're under duress. It's understandable that you'd slip up. We all make mistakes."

"I suppose, but this was a doozy." Her eyes widened, and she met his gaze. "What if he's someone related to a case you're working on?" She blew out a breath. "I would feel so much better if I didn't bring trouble to your house."

Her concern for him surprised him. "Don't worry. We'll get this figured out soon. Frank has a camera that should capture good surveillance pictures for us."

"Do I know this Frank guy?"

"Have you heard of Protection Inc.?"

"Of course. They're one of the best bodyguard and security firms in the area. Why call a bodyguard?" Confusion laced her words.

"For starters, I knew I could count on him. He's more than meets the eye. Plus, he's a former cop, he's nearby, and I trust him. Since you said no cops, he's the best I could come up with in a pinch."

She shook her head and opened her mouth as if to argue.

"Hold on. He's one of the good guys. You're going to have to learn to trust at least a couple people if you want help."

"Okay. I get it." She raised her hands palms out. "Sorry for being difficult."

Though she was hesitant to trust, he didn't think she was being overly difficult. "No problem. I'm used to far worse. How about you take a breath and close your eyes for a few minutes while we wait."

"That actually sounds nice. It's been a full day." She closed her eyes and breathed deeply a couple times. Then her eyes shot open, and she shifted to face him. "Tell me about your friend. Frank, right?"

He bit back a chuckle that she couldn't relax for more than a few seconds. "We met a couple of summers ago. I was undercover for the FBI. I can't go into detail."

"Or you'd have to kill me?" One corner of her lips turned up.

He appreciated the smile as much as he appreciated her not pushing for more information. "Good guys don't do that." His phone vibrated. He checked the screen. "Frank's here." He flicked off the kitchen light then walked to the window and watched the older man in action. To anyone who didn't know what was going on, they'd have no clue Frank was photographing the driver along with his car and license plate. He was good and staying in the shadows and not allowing himself to be seen. A moment later he darted out of the cul-de-sac presumably to his waiting car.

Trinity turned to look toward the window. "What's happening?"

"Frank got what he came for."

She parted the blind and looked out. "The car is still out there."

"Yes but not for long." Now that Frank had pictures of the man it was time to make his presence known and send him on his way. "Stay put. If you hear shots, call 9-1-1."

"Okay," she said though her voice trembled. "Are you sure you should go out there? I don't want you to get hurt because of me."

He stopped and rested a hand on her firm shoulder. "Don't worry. I'm good at my job." He gave her shoulder a light squeeze and then removed his hand. "This is what good guys do." Not that he could be her hero.

She grinned and shook her head. "Give it a rest with the good guy stuff. I know you're one of them, and I know how to recognize one when I see him."

"Glad to hear it." He stepped outside and headed toward the vehicle. The engine roared to life, and the sedan tore away. He'd hope to have a word with the man, but at least this was better than the time a perpetrator tried to run him over, and he'd had to dive out of the way. He stood on his front porch and called Frank. "Hope you did better than me."

"Got what you needed. As soon as I get back to my place, I'll send you the pictures. What's going on? I'm usually the one in need of a favor."

"I'm helping the daughter of a thief. Needless to say, she doesn't trust cops. You're the first person I could think of who was available and could operate in the shadows."

"Got it. If you need anything else…"

"Thanks." Kyle pocketed his phone as he went inside.

"I saw what happened. Now what?" He heard Trinity but couldn't see her.

He flicked on the living room lights to find her huddled in the corner of his couch with her knees drawn to her chest. She'd never looked so vulnerable. Something inside him shifted. A peace from the Lord filled him, and he determined to help her figure this gallery thing out one way or another. He sat beside her and looked straight ahead. "Now we wait. Frank will send the pictures over soon. I'll have the license plate run and also see if I can get a facial recognition hit on him."

She shifted and lowered her legs to the floor. "Really? You can do that?"

He glanced her way trying to decide if she was as surprised as she sounded. Did she really think that little of him? "It could take some time, but yes. Based on what you've told me, I'm comfortable using FBI resources to find out who was parked outside my house, clearly watching it." The FBI may or may not want this case, but it had become personal when that man invaded his sanctuary. Though he would keep that to himself, at least for now.

"When will you know something?" Trinity looked at him with anxiety-filled eyes.

"I'll get the plates run ASAP, but facial recognition

might take longer."

"Hopefully, the plates will lead us to the guy."

"Yeah." It was smart to hope for the best while preparing for the worst.

"Okay." She bit her bottom lip. "I should go."

He walked her to the door. "Do you have somewhere you can stay tonight?"

Her tone dropped. "Why?"

He leveled his gaze on her. "You're not the only person who can pick locks. You were followed here. What if he decides to do more than sit in his car?" The thought shot worry through him. She shouldn't be alone tonight. "I have a basement apartment if you want to crash there tonight."

Alarm, fear, and then resignation rested on her face. "I'll be fine." She turned the deadbolt to unlock the door before pausing with her hand on the doorknob. "Thanks for your help."

He bit his tongue as she pulled the door open. He was doing what she'd asked. And he'd warned her. What else could he do? Nothing. Yet as she slid into the night, he found himself calling her name. "Trinity."

She turned back. "Yes?"

"What's your phone number?"

There was that half smile again. The kind she might give a guy who was asking her out. Though she would know better. She rattled it off. He tapped it into his contacts list and then sent her a text so she'd have his contact info as well.

Her phone vibrated, and her eyes widened.

"You can call me if you have any more problems." He didn't like the idea of her being alone. Especially when they didn't know what was up with the driver of that sedan, but she was a grown woman capable of making decisions. "And for the record, I'll be upgrading my security system and adding a deadbolt to my backdoor."

She smiled. "Good idea." She slid her phone into her purse. "Good night."

He read people well enough to know she was only being polite and had no intention of calling if she got into trouble. He stood on the front porch watching until her taillights disappeared out of the cul-de-sac. If only she could leave his thoughts as easily.

That was the problem with being a good guy. He couldn't sleep if he knew someone was in trouble. His gut said she was in danger, and he couldn't knowingly abandon someone in need. Especially Trinity. How had that reporter managed to wiggle her way into his life? No matter. It wouldn't hurt to keep an eye on her tonight. He raced to his garage.

# 3

Trinity pulled into her apartment's numbered parking spot situated in Kirkland on the east side of Lake Washington. Home sweet home. It wasn't fancy, but it was comfortable. Before opening the door to her hatchback she looked around to make sure no one lurked. Once satisfied she was alone, she got out and hustled to her unit.

She fumbled with her key but finally managed to insert it into the lock. She pushed inside and flicked on the lights.

Cushions were strewn on the floor and chairs were on their sides. The place had been trashed.

"Oh no." She backed out of the apartment.

Agent Richards' contact info and his admonition to call him if she needed help came to mind, but she couldn't drag him further into this.

She held her breath and dialed 9-1-1. Sometimes calling the cops couldn't be helped. She strode toward her car and spotted another vehicle pulling to a stop nearby. She didn't recognize it and kept walking. She wouldn't be safe until she was locked inside her car.

Agent Richards got out of the vehicle.

She gasped.

"Everything okay?" he asked.

Here she was trying not to involve him in any deeper. Too late for that. "What are you doing here?"

He glanced toward her apartment building. "Making sure you got home okay."

Was this guy for real? She knew he didn't like her. No one in law enforcement did. She complicated their jobs by doing hers. "Seriously? I told you I would call."

He glanced at her phone. "That's not my number."

Busted. But it appeared her instincts about him held true. He was an honorable man who could be trusted. Still… "How did you know where I live?"

"I followed you." He nodded toward the door to her apartment. "What happened? Something must be really wrong for you to be calling the police."

"Someone trashed my place."

He stood taller and looked around as if watching for trouble. "I'm sorry, but good for you."

There really wasn't anything good about this situation. "I can look beyond my prejudices when it's absolutely necessary." Though calling the police didn't make her feel any safer. She reached in her pocket for her car keys.

"Where are you going?" Agent Richards asked.

"Nowhere. I can't wait for the police inside my

apartment. I don't want to disturb anything." She pressed the unlock button on her key fob and settled inside.

He slid into the passenger seat. "Looks like you need to invest in a security system as well."

She frowned, seeing her home through his eyes. The complex had seen better days, but the management made sure everything worked, so she didn't complain. There hadn't ever been a break-in before. "This is usually a safe neighborhood, even if the complex is a little rundown."

"I didn't mean to sound judgmental. I just want to make sure you're safe."

"I'll be fine. No worries." It was true that her job didn't pay a lot, considering the cost of living, but she was happy, and her car ran well. What more could she ask?

A police cruiser pulled into the lot and parked nearby.

On autopilot, she got out and waved to the responding officer. Agent Richards joined her, and even if she didn't always like him, it was nice to have a good guy on her side.

The male officer approached. "I received a call about a break-in."

"Yes." Trinity pointed to her door. "It's right there. I only stepped in then left as soon as I switched on the light."

Agent Richards flashed his badge. "I'm not on

official business, but I'm here if you need me."

The officer nodded and then headed inside.

Trinity started to follow, but Agent Richards stopped her with a hand on her arm. She looked at him and then at her arm. "What?"

He removed his hand. "Give him a minute. We don't want to interfere, especially if whoever tore up your place is lying in wait inside.

She caught her breath. "You think someone's in there?" How had that not crossed her mind?

"Anything's possible." He glanced at his watch and then toward the door again where the officer stood and motioned for them. "Looks like it's okay."

"Whew, but I think I'll wait out here just the same. I wouldn't want to crowd the police officer."

Agent Richards took her hand. "Come on. I'll protect you from the big bad police officer."

She appreciated his sense of humor, though the unexpected touch made her jumpier than flashing blue and red police lights. "My hero." She tried to keep her tone teasing while pulling her hand free and tucking it into her coat pocket.

She refused to be attracted to a law enforcement officer no matter how handsome, charming, and solicitous. The salt and pepper at his temples gave him an air of sophistication that drew her. *Don't go there, girl.*

"Trinity?" Agent Richards' questioning gaze met hers as they stood outside the front door. "I asked if you were ready to go inside."

"Oh. Sorry. My mind wandered. Yes." She stepped past him and opened the door.

The police officer strode toward them. "It appears someone was searching for something."

Trinity gasped. "What?" Why would anyone think she had something of theirs? She wasn't the thief in the family.

"I wouldn't know, ma'am. I'll dust for prints, though I'm guessing it won't do much good." He paused and looked at her face again. "I know you. You're a reporter, right?"

She raised her chin. "Yes. I assume you'll need a set of elimination prints from me."

"Yes, ma'am."

"I'll stop by the station before I head out tomorrow. Does that work?"

"That's fine."

Agent Richards cleared his throat. "Any idea how the intruder entered?"

"Looks like the slider," the officer said. "There are no broken windows, and the front door wasn't breached."

"That makes sense," Agent Richards motioned toward the balcony that was only a few feet off the ground. "May I?"

The officer nodded. "Don't touch anything before I dust for prints."

Kyle frowned and pulled blue latex gloves from his jacket pocket.

Trinity held in a chuckle. The cop seemed to have forgotten he was talking to an elite law enforcement officer. She followed him onto the balcony. "Do you see anything?"

He pointed to a dirty handprint. "Looks like he was wearing gloves. See how you can't see any striations."

She nodded. "He must have slipped in the wet grass. Isn't it unusual to be able to see a handprint with the naked eye?"

He shrugged. "Dirty hands make it easy." He turned and looked at the door. "See here. This is definitely where he entered. You need to secure this door better."

She couldn't help noticing the irony of their conversation from earlier when she'd told him the same thing about his back door. "I'll get on that tomorrow."

He nodded. "What are you going to do now?"

"What do you mean?"

"Are you staying here tonight?"

"Can I?"

"Of course. Once the officer is done, the place is all yours."

She looked at the mess and tried to squash her trepidation. She doubted a hotel would be any safer. "What are the chances he'll come back tonight?"

"It's possible. Any idea what he was looking for?"

"None, but I assume this is related to the gallery in some way. The thing is, I didn't take anything from there except the card I gave you, so what could they think I have? If I'm right about the surveillance cameras, they should know I don't have anything." Unless… "Do you think he could be after the pictures I took?"

"Can they identify anyone?"

She pulled out her phone and opened her photo app. "I have several side profile views." She handed him her phone.

"It's not the best angle."

"I know. But it's what I could get." She pointed to one man. "Don't you think he looks like the driver?"

"Yeah." He pulled out his phone and opened his text messages. He held the phones side-by-side. "He's the key to whatever's going on. We need to find him."

"I agree." The reporter in her wanted to find the man right this minute, but the rest of her never wanted to see him again. As a little girl, she used to play "do-over" and imagine what things would have been like if she could stop time and rewind after something bad happened to prevent it from happening—a dad who wasn't caught up in a life of crime, no foster homes, a mom who hadn't walked out on them. Now she wanted a do-over of last night. If she hadn't gasped and dropped her clutch, they never would have known she was there. "I thought of something. Unless they caught me on video taking their pictures, there's no way they could know I took their picture."

"Does your phone sound like a camera when you take pictures?"

"I keep my ringer on silent. I can't risk it going off while I'm live on the air." Could they have her on a surveillance video? That would sure explain things. She shook her head.

"Maybe they're guessing, or we're off base and they're after something else."

He was no help. All she had were maybes and speculation. This couldn't go on. She needed facts.

"Here's something to consider," Agent Richards said. "They know you were watching and listening, but they don't know what you heard. What if they think you heard something and maybe wrote it down?"

"I suppose, but it's a stretch." She offered a weak smile. "Thanks for trying."

The police officer joined them on the balcony and dusted the railing and door for prints, not that it would do any good. "Looks like the perpetrator wore gloves."

"We noticed," she said, surprised he hadn't figured that out already from the prints inside her apartment. "I assume you no longer need my prints for comparison."

"It's up to you, but I don't think it's necessary. I doubt any of the prints I took will be useful."

She nodded and went inside, sensing Agent Richards close behind. She turned. "Now what?"

"That's up to you. Would you like help putting this place back to rights? It shouldn't take too long with us working together since it's so small."

The police officer strode inside. "I'll be on my way. Here's my number in case you need to reach me." He handed Trinity his card and then let himself out.

Kyle picked up a throw pillow and placed it onto the sofa. "You should still leave your prints. You never know. There could have been more than one person. He might not have been as careful."

"I didn't think of that." She righted the trashcan and scooped up the rubbish that had been dumped. "He's not going to stop until he gets what he wants, is he?"

"Probably not. But my biggest concern is that he undoubtedly knows you can identify him."

Anger filled her. "I can't believe someone's going to so much trouble for stolen art. Coming after me is stupid. How can they not know that?" Unless something turned up missing from the gallery, and they thought she took it. A shiver of fear snaked through her. She was in deep trouble. She wanted the bad guys to be brought to justice but hadn't anticipated they would come after her in the process. Sure, she'd experienced a few minor incidents of retaliation like the time her tires had been slashed, but this was next level.

"There might be more than meets the eye going on," Agent Richards said. "Maybe stolen art isn't really what's being smuggled. Your informant could have been wrong. The art could be a way to smuggle drugs, or if we're truly talking about antiquities, there's a lot of money to be had there too."

What had she walked into? It was surreal that she was dealing with this considering her dad's chosen profession. He'd been known to steal art from time to time, but he mostly stuck to easy-to-fence stuff. Nothing that would interest a gallery like the Kendall Victoria.

Within an hour her apartment looked almost the way she had left it. All that needed done now was cleaning the surfaces. She dampened two rags and tossed one to Agent Richards. "I can't thank you enough for helping me tonight. You've really surprised me. I mean, I knew I could trust you, but you've proven to be a friend too. Thanks." She glanced his way as he wiped off the mantel where a vase had once sat, but now lay in pieces in the garbage.

"Whoa, don't go saying something you can't take back. You sure you can be friends with anyone in law enforcement? Seems to me it goes against some kind of personal code."

*Ouch.* She'd definitely not given him a good impression about who she was. Her heart sank and her face heated. Why did she have such a hard time showing her true self to people? This is why she was a loner. It was easier and less complicated, and she didn't risk putting her foot in her mouth. At least she could cover her flub. "I just meant that you're nicer than I expected considering I broke into your house."

"Bummer and here I thought maybe we could be friends." His gaze locked on hers. "It's clear you're in over your head. Even if it turns out I can't help in an official capacity, I want to see you through this."

Warmth flooded her body. If she wasn't careful, she might swoon. Okay, maybe not swoon. That wasn't her style, but this man was a hero whether he meant to be or not.

Agent Richards had caught her eye the first time she had run into him at the FBI months ago. He'd been walking out as she was entering. She'd asked him a question, and he had politely answered. The other agents with him had ignored her and kept walking. After that encounter, she'd made a point to dig a little bit into his life and career. Though she hadn't found much other than he'd been in the military prior to becoming an FBI agent, what she had discovered made her feel as if he was a man of integrity. His co-workers respected him. That meant a lot to her way of thinking. He was a man to be trusted. He'd proven that tonight more than once since she'd barged into his life.

He stood at the sink, rinsing the rag. And she was about to ask for more.

"Agent Richards?"

He looked over his shoulder. The sports jacket that was part of his standard FBI "uniform" had been placed over the back of her couch, and his shirtsleeves were rolled up. In a way, he reminded her of her dad who had always been good about keeping things tidy, but the two men couldn't be more different. Dad had been angry with a chip on his shoulder where Agent Richards had a peace about him, even when he'd discovered her in his house.

"I'm feeling uneasy about being here alone tonight." She'd meant to ask him to sleep on her couch, but the words got stuck in her throat. She'd see how he responded to this admission first.

He turned to face her, no question in his dark eyes, only the solemnity of understanding.

The peace that came with relief gave her courage. "I'm really not a needy person, but I'll admit to feeling vulnerable. Telling you this makes me feel pathetic too, but you know, since you're a good guy…" She smiled weakly. "Would you mind sleeping on my couch tonight?"

He just stared. She at least thought the part about him being a good guy would get a smile.

She took a bracing breath and squared her shoulders. "It's fine. Forget I asked."

"Wait." He held up a hand. "I want you to feel safe. I'm just not sure staying here is the best idea."

Relief that he was still willing to help her eased the tension in her shoulders. Sure she had friends, but she wouldn't put them in danger. "I don't have any place else to go."

He rubbed the back of his neck. "I have an idea, but you're not going to like it."

# 4

From his spot at Trinity's kitchen sink, Kyle studied her. Though she looked to be around twenty-five with her youthful-looking green eyes and fit figure, he learned on the drive over here that she had turned thirty in January. The spunky reporter had a surprisingly vulnerable side. He was beginning to think the attitude he witnessed on television was for show or perhaps a defense mechanism, because the lady standing across the room from him was not that woman. This person, though not a pushover, was scared and tried hard to hide it.

"Until we can apprehend the person who broke in here, I think you should hire someone to protect you."

She crossed her arms. "That's not an option."

"Why not?"

"I'm broke. I have a little savings, but not enough to cover what you're talking about."

He stifled a sigh. Frank's team at Protection Inc. was exactly who Trinity needed while he looked into whomever was behind her trouble. He couldn't watch her back twenty-four-seven like she needed.

"What? Your silence is disconcerting."

"I don't think you're safe here. It's too risky. I know I mentioned this before, and you turned it down, but the offer stands for you to stay in my basement apartment. At least then, I'll be close if anything happens."

"Oh." Fear flashed in her eyes for a second. She looked away. "This is unexpected. You're full of surprises, Special Agent Richards."

His face warmed. "The same can be said for you. My friends call me Kyle." He turned back to the sink and squeezed out the rag.

"We're friends?" Her soft voice was much closer now.

He stilled, draped the rag over the center of the sink, and then turned to face her. "We're getting there. If you want to stay in my basement, go pack what you need. I have an early morning and need some shuteye." He could go without sleep, but he needed to create space between them. This woman, in spite of all the trouble that seemed to follow her, had wiggled herself into his life, and he couldn't abandon her.

Trinity turned and left the room without saying anything.

He called Frank. "Hey, it's me."

"Twice in one night?"

Kyle chuckled. "Yeah, I know. Crazy. I could use your help again."

Frank was a man of integrity, and he was confident he'd assist him if he could.

"Does this mean we're working together now?" Frank only sounded half serious.

"You know I try to help you out whenever I'm able." Unfortunately, he couldn't share information unless he had permission, which he wasn't often given.

"I know, and I appreciate that. What do you need?" Frank had come to him numerous times when his clients had brought illegal activities to his attention. In fact, Frank's tip had been key in stopping bank robbers last year.

"Are you familiar with a reporter by the name of Trinity Lockhart?"

"Yes. Why?" Cautious curiosity clouded his tone.

Yep, he must be familiar with her. "She came to me for help tonight. I strongly suspect she's the reason that man was in front of my place."

"I see. Go on."

"When she arrived home this evening, she discovered her place had been ransacked. I'm taking her back to my house. I have an unoccupied basement apartment. Do you know of someone who works cheap who would be willing to watch her back during the day when I'm not available."

"Until Marc and Carissa return from their honeymoon it'll be a challenge, but we're only looking at one more day, so we can make it work."

"You're sure?" He didn't want anyone else to be in

jeopardy because of his request.

"Yes. You wouldn't ask if this wasn't important to you. I want to help. We like to look out for our friends. I know I don't speak for myself alone, but you're one of us even if you are FBI."

Kyle cleared his throat. "That means a lot. Thank you."

"If she can manage our friends and family rate we'll work out a protection detail for her. I have Sally doing research on a case, but I'll pull her off that and place her on protection duty. She doesn't work past five though, which will be a problem since my team is booked solid around the clock."

"That's fine. I'll make sure Trinity's protected after five." He'd have to cash in a favor or two to make it happen. Not the way he wanted to use those favors, but it was necessary to keep Trinity safe until he could stop whoever had ransacked her place.

"Sounds like a plan. Let me know what your friend wants to do, and I'll get everything in motion."

"You got it. Thanks. I'll be in touch. I need to get Trinity to agree to the idea." Was she really as hard up financially as she indicated? He sure hoped not.

"It sounds like her life could depend on it. Stay safe." Frank ended the call.

"Ready." Trinity walked into the room from the hallway. She held one large and one carry-on sized suitcase. She must be planning to stay awhile. He hoped it wouldn't take that long, but if it did, she appeared to be prepared.

He reached for the larger of the two bags. "I'll follow you back to my place."

Trinity stared in disbelief at the apartment below Kyle's house. It was a cave. No wonder he didn't have renters. White walls with no decoration surrounded worn parquet flooring—definitely not the beach vibe she had going on at her place. A lone, tired green couch looked forlorn in the center of the living room kitchen combo facing the tiny kitchen. A small dining table and two chairs sat in the corner between the kitchen and the door that concealed the stairs to the house above.

"I know it's not what you're accustomed to, but it's clean, and you'll be safe here. The bedroom at least has a comfortable mattress. There are extra linens in the closet."

She plastered on a smile and faced him. "It's great. Thanks." She yawned. "Sorry. It's been a day."

"Yes. It has. I'll check on you in the morning before I head out." He turned toward the door that led to the house upstairs. "I talked to my friend at Protection Inc. He offered you the friends and family discount."

She hated the idea more than she could say, but what else could she do? This person clearly was after something and wouldn't stop until he found it or until the police caught him. "I suppose I could manage a few days of protection. You don't think I'm safe at the news station?"

He shrugged. "How long are you actually there? You're in the field a lot."

She hadn't given her work routine much thought, but he wasn't wrong. "That's true. I never know where I'll be from day to day. Which will work to my advantage if someone wants to get to me. No one will know where to expect me to be at any given time."

"That means your arrival and departure will be your most exposed times. What do I tell Frank?"

The answer was obvious though it was the last thing she wanted. She had some savings, but it would go fast if she guessed even close to the cost of hiring a bodyguard. She sighed. "Fine. But only for a few days if he expects to get paid."

Kyle studied her face a moment as if trying to read her thoughts. "Okay. I'll get things in motion." He turned and departed through the stairwell that led to the main level.

Thankfulness filled her. Who knew he'd prove to be such a prince? She headed into the bedroom with her luggage and plopped onto the bed. If someone had told her yesterday she'd be taking refuge in the home of a law enforcement officer today, she'd have laughed and told them they didn't know her at all.

Life had changed quickly. On one hand, she wished she'd ignored the tip, but a bigger part of her wanted to know what was going on and to be a part of taking down the traffickers.

Unease made her chest hurt. She needed to get a

grip on this tension before she landed in the hospital. She reached for her phone and opened her photo app. The profile of the man shone on the screen. "Who are you, and what do you want with me?"

Trinity startled awake. Where was she? She looked at the drop ceiling above her and then to the right at an unadorned white wall—Kyle's basement. The place seriously needed a makeover, but like he'd said, the mattress had been comfortable, so she had no complaints. She'd slept deeply and felt surprisingly rested for being in a strange place.

Beauty sleep was a key component to keeping her job secure. She needed to look her best or some beautiful younger woman might come along and snag her position from under her.

She slid out from beneath the sheets and padded into the main living area and headed for the kitchen in hopes of finding coffee. A person sat at the table. She stifled a scream. Her heart pounded. "May I help you?"

A woman whipped around to face her. "I hope I didn't scare you." The medium-build brunette with wavy hair to her shoulders stood and offered her hand. "I'm Sally Wilson, your bodyguard for the day. Kyle let me in."

Trinity took her hand and gave it a firm shake or at least the best she could do considering she'd awakened only moments ago. "It's nice to meet you. I'm Trinity Lockhart." She would have to have a word with Kyle about letting people into the apartment when she was sleeping. Then again, this was payback for breaking into his place. She probably should let it slide. "He didn't tell me to expect you."

Sally's hazel eyes widened. "Oh. I'm sorry, I didn't realize. I work for Protection Inc. hence the bodyguard statement."

Trinity chuckled in spite of everything. "I kind of figured. Thanks for coming. I didn't know someone would be here so early."

Sally smiled warmly. "You're welcome. I imagine after what you've been though, waking up to a stranger outside your bedroom would be disconcerting at the least." She waved a hand. "Kyle said to tell you he'll touch base later."

"Okay. Thanks." She owed the man big time for everything he'd done to help her. She bit down on her bottom lip. If she had a bodyguard in place before sunup, Protection Inc. must believe, based on what Kyle told them, that she was in imminent danger. She shivered. It was as if a dark threat hovered over her head, but she didn't know where it was.

"You cold?"

"Not really, but I am freaked out. It occurred to me that Kyle truly thinks I'm in danger. Seeing you here made it all very real."

Sally nodded. "Kyle is a good friend to the owners at Protection Inc., and he's always there when we need him. My bosses trust him, so your assessment is on target. I'm sorry."

Trinity nodded then opened one cupboard after another. No coffee. "That's a problem."

"What?" Sally asked.

"No coffee. We need coffee." She glanced up.

Sally stood. "Kyle said to help ourselves upstairs. I'll make us some while you get dressed. I see why Kyle likes you."

If only. "He doesn't like me. He's just a nice guy with a hero complex and can't help himself from saving a damsel in distress."

Sally returned to the table and sat. "I'll let you keep believing that if you want to, but he didn't call you a damsel in distress. He called you trouble. Which is something he usually tries to steer clear of. As for being a hero?" She shrugged. "Though he is, he does *not* have a hero complex. Kyle is very down to earth. I'm surprised by your accusation."

Trinity sat in a chair across from Sally. "Oh." Maybe her biases clouded her opinion. "I didn't mean to offend. I'm sorry if I did." Talk about getting off to a rocky start. Not the way she wanted things to go when she met her bodyguard. "Do you ever wish you could rewind your life and take a different path?"

"I can understand the sentiment, but no. I wouldn't be who I am without the choices I've made. My life is the cumulation of my experiences."

Trinity propped her elbow on the table and rested her chin in her hand. "I suppose you're right." She stood. "Please excuse me, while I get ready for work."

Thirty minutes later, she found Sally exactly where she'd left her, only this time she held a steaming mug of coffee. A second mug sat on the table.

"I brought you down a cup. I didn't know how you take it. It's black and pretty strong."

"Black is fine. Thanks." Trinity walked over to the table, grasped the warm mug, and then sat across from her bodyguard. She breathed in the heavenly scent of hazelnut, took a sip, and grinned. Kyle had good taste. "How does this bodyguard thing work?"

Sally sat a little taller and straightened her broad shoulders. "I'll stick with you wherever you go until five tonight."

She wasn't off work until after the six o'clock news. "What happens at five?"

"Kyle will meet you at the station and follow you home unless you would rather I drive. In which case, he would bring you back here."

Trinity took another sip of the coffee. She was going to need it even with sleeping so well. "It'd be better if we only had one car to park."

"Then I'll drive." Sally stood and rinsed her mug in the sink. "How long until you're ready to leave?"

"That depends. Are you a breakfast person?"

Sally grinned. "Favorite meal of the day, and I've missed it two days in a row. My daughter had a meltdown this morning."

It was weird to think her bodyguard had a life outside of protecting Trinity. But as she knew from work, everyone had a story. She didn't want to get in Sally's way. "I'm sorry. Was it because of me?"

Sally shook her head. "No. She didn't like what I made her for breakfast and tipped the entire bowl onto the floor while in the midst of a tantrum. We both went without food. Something tells me she won't do that again."

Trinity felt for both mom and daughter. "How old is she?"

"Three. Her adoption finally went through in December. Her mom and I were close, so it's bittersweet."

"Her mom died?"

Sally nodded once and brought the cup to her lips.

"I'm sorry." That poor baby would never know her mother. At least she had someone like Sally who could tell her all about her birth mom.

"Thanks. It's been a challenge, but we're finding a rhythm. When Bethany asked me to be Emma's godmother, I was honored, but to be honest, I never dreamed I'd end up raising my best friend's daughter. Just goes to show you never know."

Trinity winced at the morbid turn their conversation had taken. Death was not something she cared to think about. She gulped down the rest of the coffee, wishing she had time to savor it, but if she was going to treat Sally to breakfast before work, she needed to move. "I'll be right back. There's a great mom and pop diner on the way to the news station. I can't have my bodyguard faint from hunger."

Sally chuckled. "Kyle didn't mention how thoughtful you are."

Trinity smiled ruefully. "I don't imagine he's aware." She rushed into the tiny bathroom and brushed her teeth then headed to the door where Sally waited.

"I need to make sure everything looks safe outside. Wait here." Sally strode out the door.

Trinity stood on tiptoes watching from the high, narrow window as the woman looked under her car then scanned the area. She headed toward the door. Trinity went to the door and waited.

The door opened. "We're clear. Stay close and do exactly as I say."

"Yes, ma'am." She hadn't seen this side of the woman yet and was glad they'd met in a more relaxed setting first. Her pulse accelerated, and she tried to stay calm even though every instinct in her said to run and hide.

A minute later, they were driving out of the cul-de-sac. Sally glanced her way. "You did good. Breathe."

Trinity blew out a breath. "That was intense."

"You'll get used to it."

"Somehow, I doubt that. How do you do this day in and day out?"

"To be honest, I don't. My job varies more than the rest of the team."

"Why's that?" Trinity shook her head. "I'm going into reporter mode again. I have a habit of asking a lot of questions."

"It's fine. As for your question, I'm good at research, so I'm often tasked with that instead of protection duty. But don't worry. I spend a good deal of time protecting people too."

Trinity nodded. "How'd you come to work for Protection Inc.?"

"I was a burned-out cop in need of a change. The rest is history." Sally glanced in the rearview mirror and frowned. "Looks like we might have a tail. Hang on." She swerved across two lanes and then made a fast right.

Trinity chanced a look over her shoulder. She didn't see the car from last night or anyone tailgating them. "Are they still there?"

Both hands on the wheel, Sally accelerated through a yellow light. She braked hard, pulled into a small parking lot, and then stopped one row back, behind parked vehicles. They sat in silence for what seemed like five minutes, but in reality, it was probably no more than two. "I think we lost him. To be safe, we'll sit here a bit longer."

A moment later, a car that looked like the sedan parked outside of Kyle's house last night drove past the lot. Trinity sucked in a sharp breath. "That's him. I didn't see him at the house. How'd he find us?"

"Good question. Have you considered using a few sick days? You're going to be an easy target at the news station."

Trinity whipped her gaze toward Sally. "No. Do

you really think that's necessary?" She could probably take a sick day or two but really didn't want to use them unless she was actually sick. It was a moral issue for her. Then again, she could always take a mental health day in good conscience. This was definitely stressful.

"This dude isn't messing around. He clearly knows where you're staying. We can assume he knows where you work. How good is security at the news station?"

"It could be better." If that man wanted to get to her at work, he'd have little problem. Sure, they had a security guard, but Trinity watched enough TV to know that wouldn't stop him if he was determined to get to her. "Now what do we do?"

"Breakfast?" Sally's stomach growled.

"Sounds good to me. We only lost a few minutes. The diner is nearby. We could park here and walk if you'd like."

"Is there a closer lot?"

Trinity nodded.

"Then that's where we'll go. You're too vulnerable out in the open."

Trinity gave Sally directions and then kept her gaze trained on the passenger side-view mirror. What if the man found them again? Would she ever be safe? Would she be better off facing him to find out exactly what he was after?

They managed to find close parking, had a quick but delicious meal of pancakes and eggs, and then headed to the station.

"I'll stay in the background," Sally said. "Tell your co-workers as much or as little as you want."

"Got it. So don't introduce you to anyone?"

"It's not necessary unless it is." Sally grinned.

Even with all the curious stares from her co-workers, the morning flew by. She filled in her boss on the situation and explained it had to do with a story she was working on. She finally pitched the art smuggling story idea to Clancy, and he loved it. To her surprise, the station offered to pick up the cost of her protection while she worked the story. It felt good that she was so valued, but on the other hand, it was disconcerting to need protection at all.

Promptly at five, Sally left. Trinity had to be on air during the five o'clock news, so she didn't get a chance to say good-bye. Supposedly, Kyle was in the building, but she was too busy to figure out where.

She finally got back to her desk at six twenty following her live shot and closed her eyes. What a day.

"Hi." The deep masculine voice woke her up quicker than her alarm clock.

She looked up from her computer to find Kyle standing beside her desk. Her heart skipped a beat. "Hey. How was your day?"

"Busy. I heard you ran into some trouble on your way here."

She winced at the memory. "Yeah. I'm thankful Sally was driving, but it was pretty scary. You should've seen her. The way she careened through traffic and lost him. It was impressive."

"She's had good training. You ready to get out of here?"

Trinity nodded. "Where have you been? Sally said you were taking over at five, but I haven't seen you until now."

"Sorry about that. I had to deal with something at work and couldn't get away. I had a friend keep an eye on you in my absence." He motioned toward a woman sitting along the wall and holding a magazine. Trinity hadn't noticed before.

"Who's that?"

"Another agent."

The female agent stood and sauntered over to them. "Consider my debt paid." She left without another word.

Trinity raised a brow. "You sure she's a friend?"

He frowned as his gaze trailed after her. "Yeah, but she feels the same way about reporters as you do about cops."

"Ouch." It wasn't fair, but wasn't she doing the same thing with regard to cops? "You might want to do something nice for her tomorrow." She stood and gathered her stuff. They walked out of the station and to his car. Trinity pondered the sudden influx of law enforcement in her life and how each had stepped up beyond what she expected. Her dad had reason to not trust cops considering his chosen profession, but maybe, just maybe, he'd misjudged them too. She settled beside Kyle as he pulled into traffic. "I have good news."

"What's that?" He glanced in the rearview mirror but didn't appear to be overly concerned about anything.

She checked over her shoulder too. No familiar cars followed. "My boss said the station would pay for my security."

He shot her a sideways glance. "Can you hire who you want, or was he talking about the guard in the lobby?"

"Sally quoted him a price, and he agreed."

"I didn't expect that."

"Me neither." That was an understatement. She'd been shocked.

"Sally checked in with me earlier. It seems the two of you got along well. She talked to Frank about staying on as your protection during the day."

"And…"

"Frank reluctantly agreed since he pulled her from another project, but he thought it might be good if you had an additional bodyguard."

That didn't sound good. "Why? Am I really in that much danger?" Other than being followed, no one had tried to harm her.

"That's the problem, we don't know. The plates on the car we spotted outside my house last night were stolen from another vehicle. I'm still working on finding him though. Looks like your tip about the gallery might have some substance too. If those traffickers are onto you…"

A shiver shot through her. Those dudes looked mean. She wouldn't want to encounter either of them alone, but Sally would have to be enough. "I don't want a second bodyguard. Plus, I'm certain the station wouldn't cover the cost, and I'm not inclined to do it either."

"That's unfortunate."

This was all so surreal. "I'm probably the last person you ever thought you'd be helping."

"Not the last, but close." He chuckled. "I know how reporters are about giving up their sources, but I'm hoping in light of all that's happened, you'll tell me the name of yours. Whoever tipped you off about the art gallery might know something to help put a stop to the people behind your trouble."

"If I knew, I'd tell you. It came in as an anonymous tip."

He glanced her way. "Is that normal?"

She shrugged. "It happens."

"Seems like a security risk to me." He signaled and turned.

"Doesn't the FBI follow up on all tips, including anonymous ones?"

"You're not the FBI."

"But I have an obligation to our viewers." They entered his neighborhood.

"You could've reported the tip to the authorities

and stayed out of harm's way."

"I could have, but then we wouldn't be having this delightful discussion." She couldn't help the sarcasm. She was wired to follow the story, and that's what she did.

He pulled into his garage. "Home sweet home."

Trinity got out without saying a word. Though the day had gone by quickly, she was ready for it to end. "Good night." She walked toward the driveway.

"Where are you going?" He followed her to the edge of the garage.

"The apartment."

"Use the inside entrance. It's not safe for you to be out there in the open." He lowered the garage door. His chocolate-colored eyes softened as their gazes met.

Her stomach flopped. She'd always loved chocolate, but this reaction to him had to stop. Right now.

She could never be in a relationship with someone in law enforcement. Sure, she had once wanted to be in the FBI, but she wasn't FBI quality. Their rejection when she applied to the bureau proved that. But Kyle was different. He hadn't rejected her when she'd come to him. *Stop.* Allowing her mind to fixate on him was a bad idea.

"Please wait for me to enter the house first. We both know this place has at least one vulnerability."

Her cheeks warmed. Note to self—never break into an FBI agent's house again. "About that. I'm really sorry."

"Surprisingly, I'm not." He brushed past her and entered his home. "Wait here while I clear the rooms." A few minutes later, he went down the stairs leading to her apartment.

She kept her gaze fixed on the stairwell. He'd been down there several minutes. She rubbed the small of her back to ease the ache that had formed. Where was he? The apartment wasn't large, and it didn't have a bunch of places for a bad guy to hide.

She shifted from one foot to the next. Her feet were killing her. She kicked off the heels she'd put on this morning. They were comfortable enough for on-air shots if needed, but she'd been standing too long. What was taking him so long?

The ticking on the clock broke into her thoughts. Something wasn't right. She tiptoed to the stairs and headed down.

Kyle spoke to someone, but she could only hear Kyle's voice. Who was he talking to? She eased the door open and poked her head in. She gasped. The cushions from the couch had been sliced and the filling strewn about the space. The table chairs were on their sides, and the table had been upended. Not even one drawer was still where it belonged in the kitchenette. The apartment was in shambles, which was saying a lot considering how sparsely it was furnished.

Kyle whirled around holding his gun.

She raised her hands. "Don't shoot."

"I told you to wait upstairs." He put the gun in his

holster. "I'll see you when you get here," he said into the phone, then turned his attention to Trinity. "One of my colleagues will be here any minute to process this mess."

She took in the space. "I'm so sorry. I never imagined this would happen."

The grim look on his face softened. "Don't beat yourself up. I know you didn't mean for this to happen."

"What can I do to help?"

"Nothing right now." He rubbed the back of his neck. "Someone made a big mistake today. Breaking into a federal agent's home was a huge error in judgement."

A knock sounded on the apartment door.

Kyle checked the peep hole then opened the door. "Thanks for coming." He motioned between the man and Trinity. "Charlie, meet Trinity. Charlie is FBI and a friend. He's the person I said was on his way."

"Hi." Trinity tried to sound friendly. She'd had a run in with Charlie on live TV when she'd questioned the FBI's findings about a case he was in charge of. He'd made it clear she wasn't someone he cared for.

The clean-cut man glowered at her. "Looks like trouble is your middle name."

Her body shook. "I'm so sorry." She reached down to pick up stuffing from the couch that littered the floor. "What's the bedroom look like?"

Kyle tilted his head to the side. "Pretty much the

same. I'm afraid you'll need to go home for more clothes."

"He knifed those too?" Anger surged through her. "If only I knew what he was looking for."

"I understand. Go back upstairs. I'll be there when I can. Leave the stairwell doors open so I can hear if there's trouble."

As if her feet had a mind of their own, she traversed the stairs and sank onto the couch. She'd caused this. She rested her head in her hands. Trouble. It seemed the name suited her. Maybe her dad was right about things after all. She'd almost come to think he'd been mistaken about people in law enforcement, but the venom that Charlie spewed proved her dad correct. She couldn't stay here. But where should she go?

# 5

"Thanks, Charlie." Kyle clapped the shoulder of his closest friend at the FBI. They'd met at Quantico and had both been assigned to Seattle—Special Agent Davis was a blessing he thanked God for frequently.

"No problem. What's the deal with the reporter? I can't believe you let her stay here. You know she's trouble."

"I do, but she had nowhere else to go." Right now, she was upstairs waiting for him to finish up down here. "I thought she'd be safer here than on her own."

"You're a saint, but it looks like no matter where she is, whoever's behind this will find her."

"I think you're right. For the record, Trinity isn't bad." He was as surprised as his friend to hear those words come from his mouth. Before yesterday, he never would have uttered them.

"You mean to tell me there's a human inside that snake skin?"

He tamped the irritation that shot through him. "What'd she do to you?" Kyle eyed his friend. There had to be a story, because Charlie was one of the best-natured people he knew.

"Her reporting cost me a week's worth of work. She doesn't know when to keep her mouth shut. Had the public so riled up..." Charlie shook his head. "I don't want to talk about it."

"Okay." A lame response, but what else could he say? "I'm sure she didn't mean to cause you trouble."

Charlie raised a brow. "She's not your responsibility. What gives? I know you aren't a fan of the woman. Or at least you weren't."

His friend knew him well, but perhaps not as well as he'd thought. "I felt bad for her, and I didn't want her out there on her own. Both places she's stayed have now been ransacked. Clearly, they think she has something they want. What happens when they get even more desperate and go after her?"

"I hear you," Charlie said. "Someone is looking for something, that's for sure, and I agree. It could get dangerous if they get desperate."

"Which is why I had facial recognition run on a photo of the suspect. I'm waiting on the results."

"I don't know how you got that approved."

"Cashed in a favor."

"Of course you did. Sounds like you didn't hear though."

"Hear what?" Kyle had kept his phone on him nonstop so he wouldn't miss anything.

"Your perpetrator isn't in the system."

"You're kidding. How's that possible?"

"My guess is he's good at not getting caught," Charlie said. "Or he kills any witnesses."

Kyle frowned. "He'll have to get through me and Protection Inc. to get to Trinity. She might have rubbed us both the wrong way, but I'm telling you, she's not who I thought she was."

"I'm glad to hear it since this has become personal for you. Has she considered laying low and leaving town for a while?" Charlie packed up his equipment.

"I doubt it."

"It might be a good idea until we can figure this out." Charlie studied him for a second.

He hated that look of judgment in his buddy's eyes. He raised his chin. "Just spit it out."

Charlie shrugged. "You've accumulated a lot of vacation time. Maybe now would be a good time to use it."

"And miss out on this? No, thanks. You know I enjoy the hunt."

"Yeah, but you don't want to become the hunted. You've been dragged into something that's messy. He was in your home. Did you notice he only tore up the apartment?" Charlie motioned around the room. "I'm not kidding about talking her into leaving town. It would be the best thing for both of you. See you tomorrow." He opened the door and left.

Charlie made a good point, but for reasons that eluded him, Kyle didn't want Trinity to leave. He wanted her right here where he could watch out for her. No wonder Marc turned down the FBI when they'd tried to recruit him—protecting others gave a sense of fulfillment that working for the FBI didn't give him. He'd noticed the same when he'd worked with the team in Lincoln City, Oregon. Technically, he had been on the job for the FBI, but his cover was to work with the Protection Inc. team. He'd enjoyed it too, until everything went haywire.

Trinity stood at the bottom of the stairs. She looked in from the doorway. "It's just me. I'm really sorry about all of this. I heard your friend leave. May I come in now?"

"Yes. We've processed the scene."

She stepped into the space. "I couldn't help overhearing your conversation. I'd understand if you want me to leave. You don't need me complicating your life."

He wished she hadn't heard, but it was too late now. "It's true I wasn't happy to find you in my living room last night, but—"

"I apologized."

He hadn't meant to make her feel bad again. He waved off her comment. "That's not my point. Even though I was angry at first, I'm glad you sought me out. I did some digging today, and I believe you stumbled onto something big. I can't share any details, but the

FBI is involved. I think you could be an asset. I don't want you to leave."

Interest and excitement shone in her eyes. "I'd love the exclusive on this story."

"It's your story to tell, but I'd ask you to wait until we finish the operation. If anything shows up in the media before then, it would ruin any chance we have of shutting down the art theft."

She nodded. "I understand. You have my word, but my boss is aware of what I'm working on. I can't stop him from breaking the story."

"Don't give him anything, and you shouldn't have a problem."

"The station is paying for the cost of my protection."

"Does the protection come with strings?" He wouldn't put it past her boss.

She shrugged. "Not officially but I feel obligated. Plus, it's my story, and I want to break it."

He nodded. "I don't see that being a problem unless there's a leak at the news station."

"No one would dare."

He took a breath and blew it out slowly as he looked around at the mess. Good thing this apartment was sparse to begin with, but he'd have to invest in a new sofa and bed. "One thing is clear to me. He thinks you have something. Are you sure you didn't take anything?"

"Only the pictures on my phone and the business

card I picked up from the floor."

"I don't think the pics are what he's after. He has to know by now you turned them over to the authorities. There must be something else."

"I can't imagine what it is. I strolled through the gallery. Spoke with only a few people—"

His head jerked toward her. "You didn't mention that before. Who'd you talk to?"

"The gallery owner, the ticket collector, and a man who was admiring a photograph."

He frowned. They had yet to determine if the gallery owner was involved. Based on what he had gleaned so far, the owner's assistant was more than likely the one behind the art theft ring. "Tell me about the man."

"Honestly, I barely noticed him. I was trying to blend in. The owner honed in on me right away." She closed her eyes. "The man was probably in his middle thirties. He had dark short-cropped hair, and he wore a tux."

"Fancy."

"It was black-tie. He looked like everyone else that night."

He stifled a sigh. "How'd you get in since it was by invitation only?"

She shrugged. "I flashed my press badge."

"That worked?" He shouldn't be surprised, but a part of him was.

"I got in, didn't I?"

"Right." It had been a long day, and they weren't getting anywhere. "I have a frozen dinner with your name on it if you're interested."

"I thought I'd have something delivered."

He shook his head. "Too risky."

Her shoulders sagged.

His heart softened a bit more toward the woman. Before yesterday, he'd only seen the reporter. Now he hurt for the woman behind the façade. "Maybe I can get someone I trust to help us."

"Frozen food is fine. I don't expect to be here so long it will rot my insides."

He chuckled. He sure hoped not. "I didn't realize you were a health nut. Do you cook? I sure wouldn't turn down a home-cooked meal."

"Not really, but I try to eat healthy foods as often as possible."

He headed up the stairs and heard her footfalls on the steps behind him. He'd try and stop by the grocery store tomorrow for fresh food. "So, you don't cook at all?"

"A little. Honestly, by the time I get home from work, I'm too tired to put in much effort, so I usually eat a salad that I made over the weekend."

That explained her trim figure. "What about protein?"

"I add seeds, nuts, and sometimes fish or chicken. It depends on my mood."

He took the last stair and headed straight for the kitchen.

"What's the plan?" Trinity sat on a barstool.

He pulled open the freezer and pulled out the last of his frozen meals. "I pop these in the microwave, and *voilà*, we have food."

She chuckled. "I meant about stopping the man who keeps trashing everywhere I've been. We both know he's going to come after me next, assuming he didn't find what he's looking for."

He had wondered how long it would take for her to come to that conclusion. "Let the FBI handle this, Trinity. You'll be safe with Protection Inc. and me watching your back." At least that was his prayer. Even if she annoyed his coworkers, he didn't want her hurt. He hated the idea of something happening to her. If only they could figure out what the man was after.

Trinity admired Kyle's broad shoulders and breathed a sigh of relief that she had someone like him watching out for her. "When this is all over, I'll take you to dinner. Anywhere you want to go."

He glanced over his shoulder and raised a brow. "That's an intriguing offer."

She grinned and ducked her chin. Did he really just flirt? She had to have imagined it. "Any idea where you'd want to go?"

He turned and leaned against the counter near the microwave. "I'll have to give it some thought. I hate to harp on the same thing over and over, but are you sure you didn't leave with anything from the gallery?"

She blew out a breath. She'd asked the same question numerous times. She closed her eyes, envisioning that night. "I walked in and spotted the business card. I bent down to pick it up and someone bumped into me."

He pushed off the counter and stood. "Wait. Someone bumped into you. You didn't mention that before."

She shrugged. "It didn't seem important. Come to think of it, the man I stood beside after I left the employee area was the same man who bumped into me."

"What were you wearing?"

"A long wool coat, a black dress and heels. Why?"

"He might have slipped something into your coat pocket. Where's the coat now?"

"The back of my car."

"Key?" He opened his hand palm up.

She pulled it from her purse and tossed it to him. "I parked around the corner."

"Okay. Watch the food. I'll be right back." He strode to the door and then vanished into the darkness.

Wouldn't she have noticed if someone had dropped something into her pocket?

The microwave dinged. She stood and removed the first meal, then added the next one and pressed start.

The front door opened. "Check this out." Kyle held out a slip of paper. "Is it yours?"

She moved closer to get a better look. "A dry-cleaning receipt? No. I've never heard of that place."

"This might be what he's looking for." Excitement filled his voice.

The microwave dinged. She moved and pulled the food out. "To what end?"

"I don't know for sure, but I think it's what we needed to get this investigation rolling."

She hoped he was right but wasn't convinced a dry cleaner's receipt was worth so much trouble. "Why not leave the receipt out where he can easily see it, like on the seat of my car and then follow him? See what he does."

"Two problems. One, he'd damage your car to get it, and two, we'd risk losing him and this lead."

"But if we let him have it, he'll leave me alone."

He shook his head. "We don't know for sure this is what he's after."

"What else could it be? I've never seen that receipt before, so it stands to reason that's what he's after."

Kyle moved into the kitchen and pulled two forks from a drawer. He slid the lasagna to her.

She tilted her head. "How'd you know I'd want the lasagna?"

"Lucky guess. I think you should sleep up here tonight since everything in the apartment was destroyed."

She winced. "You mean to tell me he sliced up the mattress too?"

"Afraid so."

"Will your insurance cover the damage? If not, I will. Though it will have to be in monthly installments." She'd be paying him for years unless she picked up a side job.

"Don't worry about it."

But she did. His house was broken into because of her. Clearly, she needed to move on, but where should she go? Was any place safe?

Kyle placed a bed pillow and a couple of blankets onto the couch. "Sleep well, Trinity." He clicked off the kitchen light and headed down the hall.

A small lamp lit the living room with a moody glow. It suited her mood. Today had been a day for sure, but she wasn't ready to sleep. She reached for one of the outdoor magazines on the end table and thumbed through it.

Around midnight, her eyes finally felt heavy with sleep. She curled up on the couch and her phone rang. She picked it up and noted it was forwarded from her work phone. "Hello?"

"Be in the alley behind the gallery no later than 3:00 AM," the distorted voice said. "Bring a camera. You'll have all the evidence you need to destroy Kendall. Don't let me down."

"Are you saying stolen art is being delivered?"

"You're smart. Don't let me down."

"Wait. Who are you?"

The line went dead.

# 6

Trinity stared at the phone for a long while after the informant's call. She allowed her gaze to wander to the hallway that led to Kyle's room. If the tip panned out, she could return all the favors Kyle had done for her by solving the mystery and giving him the scoop instead. For now, though, he didn't need the burden of a woman with a target on her back, especially when she was willing to take this type of risk.

Two hours later, she stood and grabbed her coat, thankful he'd brought it from her car. She held it over her head since rain pounded the ground. No one should be awake at this time of the morning, much less going on a stake out.

Lightning lit the sky. She glanced toward Kyle's house, and her breath caught in her lungs. Leaving Kyle asleep was for the best.

She slid behind the wheel of her hatchback. The engine purred to life. "Here goes nothing." Thankfully, the car that had been following her for the past two days was nowhere in sight. Maybe the man had given up on finding the dry-cleaning receipt. Her informant said merchandise was being moved this morning. She'd swing by the news station for a camera and a change of clothes and then head over to the gallery before the action was supposed to happen.

A rap hit her window. She jerked her head to the left.

*Kyle.*

Frustration shot through her. She lowered the window a crack. Rain splashed inside hitting her in the face.

"What are you doing?" He stood with arms crossed and grimly looking down at her.

"How'd you know I was leaving?" she asked and then pressed her lips together.

He shook his head. "I thought you wanted my help. How can I help if we don't trust one another?"

Not an answer. She sucked in a breath and blew it out. "I received a tip that might be valuable, and I wanted to make it up to you for all the trouble I caused."

"Don't cut me out. An old couch and mattress are nothing compared to your life. What were you thinking?" Frustration filled his voice.

She sighed. "Fine. Get in."

"Nuh-uh." He pulled the driver's side door open. "I'll drive."

"What? Why?"

"Because right now, I don't trust you to not drive off the second I try to get to the passenger side."

The nerve. She raised herself over the center console instead of getting out and going around. She didn't care to get any more wet than she already was from the deluge. "For the record, I wasn't going to ditch you. But since you probably know some fancy driving like Sally does, you can drive in case we run into trouble." She raised her chin and crossed her arms.

Kyle sat with his hands on the wheel.

"What are you waiting for?" Trinity asked. "You do know how to drive a stick, don't you?"

"Of course. Where are we going?"

"The news station. I want to pick up an infrared camera."

"We're going on a stakeout?" His brow wrinkled.

"I suppose we are."

"You're interfering with official FBI business." He put the car in drive and pulled away from the curb.

"Since you're FBI, I don't see how that's possible now. Is the Bureau aware that art is being moved this morning?"

"I'm not at liberty to confirm or deny that information."

She shook her head. "My source said to be in place no later than three. If you don't drive faster, we'll be late and possibly blow the whole thing."

"Assuming your source is correct."

"He was last time."

"He? You failed to mention that before."

"Did I?" She honestly couldn't remember what she'd told him. Her life had been turned upside down, and she was stressed.

"What else have you failed to mention?" Kyle's grip tightened on the steering wheel.

"Nothing that I can think of." Why did he always assume she was hiding something? Maybe it came with being an FBI agent—always suspicious. "Oh yeah, when my informant called with this tip, I tried to get him to tell me who he was, but he hung up on me."

"Hmm. I'm not sure what to think about that." Kyle's face shone from the light of the streetlamps as he shot a troubled look in her direction. "Any idea why he wants to remain anonymous?"

"Not a clue. I do have a theory though." She wasn't as careless as he thought. She hadn't jumped up right away. Instead, she'd given steady thought to what she might be walking into. "He seems to be very eager for the art traffickers to be stopped. As if it's personal. Even mentioned Kendall by name. He said they needed to be stopped, and he was counting on me."

"Hmm. What else did he say?"

"That was it. I asked him who he was and then he hung up."

"You sure?"

She clenched her hands into fists at her sides. "I'm telling the truth. I'm not in the habit of lying." She'd left that trait to her dad.

"But you do seem to leave things out."

"Not on purpose. As for this morning, he called me around midnight. You were in bed. I really didn't want to trouble you any more than I have already."

"Okay. I believe you, but in the future, trouble me." His tone suggested he believed her.

She chuckled in spite of the tension in the car. "You might regret asking me to trouble you."

"I'll take my chances." He pulled into a parking garage near the news station. "I'll go with you."

She expected nothing less. At least the intruder hadn't destroyed her keycard since she kept it on her at all times. They headed inside, and she went straight to her cubicle where she kept a spare outfit. "Let me change out of yesterday's clothes. Then I'll check out the equipment."

"It's quiet. Where is everyone?"

"In an hour, this room will be buzzing. Let's move." She slipped into the ladies' restroom and quickly changed out of yesterday's outfit and into a pair of black slacks and a jewel toned blue sweater. She stuffed her dirty clothes into the bag and then rushed out.

Kyle stood to the left of the door. "That was fast."

"Mmhm." She would re-do her makeup later. She strode over to the equipment room and checked out the camera, and then they headed to the parking garage.

"Where to now?" Kyle asked.

"The gallery."

"I should've known."

Kyle studied the alley with only one way in or out and no place to hide unless they hid in plain sight. He didn't like it one bit. Yet somehow, Charlie and Paige, his FBI team, had managed to blend in. Kyle had played it coy, but thankfully, they'd intercepted the phone conversation between Trinity and her informant. He'd hoped she would come to him, but when he'd heard her sneaking out, he'd known she had no intention of keeping him in the loop.

Kyle raised the hood of his sweatshirt over his head and slid low on the cloth seat of Trinity's car. "We need to be in that alley when they arrive."

Trinity shifted beside him in her car. "How do you propose we do that?"

"See that dumpster?"

"No way! I'm not dressed for dumpster diving."

"It's the only way for us to get close enough."

"And what if they decide to use the dumpster?"

"We'll wing it."

A homeless couple, which he suspected was his team, slept at the edge of the alley under an eave.

"Fine. I can't believe I let you talk me into this." She mumbled something unintelligible, but the gist was there—she was very unhappy with their situation.

He chuckled, trying to ignore his aversion to what they were about to do. "I'm sure it's not the first time you dumpster dove."

She snapped her head in his direction. "What makes you say that?"

"Based on the childhood you described, I figured…" He let the words die on his lips. The look on her face would silence the toughest of the tough. "Sorry. I shouldn't have said that. If you want this on film, we need to get into position."

"I understand, but I really don't want to. If I had known I'd be in a dumpster, I would have waited to change into fresh clothes. It's my only nice outfit. This stinks."

"Sure will." They'd more than likely reek for days. "You ready?" He made sure the dome light wouldn't turn on, drawing attention to them.

"I guess. Let's get this over with." She opened the door.

They shot across the street.

As they passed the homeless couple with large black trash bags draped around them, Charlie made eye contact with Kyle but didn't speak. Paige looked to actually be asleep as she rested her head on Charlie's shoulder. He really did owe her after asking her to watch Trinity and then dragging her out in the wee hours of a cold and stormy morning to sit outside in the elements.

He raised the lid on the compost dumpster and jerked his head to the side. The smell of rotting food from the café next door to the gallery permeated the air.

This would be worse than he'd thought. "I'll give you a boost."

Trinity shook her head. "No way. Not happening. I am not getting in there. It smells horrible."

The hum of a nearby engine approached. "Suit yourself. Good luck." He hoisted himself over the side and cringed as something wet soaked into his sneakers.

"Kyle," she hissed. "You can't leave me here."

He stood and raised the lid and reached a hand down to assist her.

She grasped it, and a moment later, she sunk beside him. "This is the most disgusting thing I've ever done for a story."

The engine stopped. He pushed up the dumpster lid only enough to see out. Two men knocked on the garage door for the gallery. The door slid up revealing a woman. "Look at this," he whispered.

She hunched over beside him.

"Do you recognize her?"

"No, but I'm not surprised. That's not the woman who was at the exhibit. She said her name was Alexis, and she was the hostess. I think she's the owner."

His intel had brought up a driver's license photo of dark-haired Kendall Victoria, and that photo matched the woman he was looking at. Alexis had to be Kendall's assistant.

"I'm regretting this camera now," she said. "It's too big, and I can't set it down in here."

Trinity's voice was so low, he almost missed her

words, but thankfully, he didn't. He pulled out his phone and positioned it to be able to record the scene that played out in front of them. The building was lit and provided plenty of light for recording all the action.

He frowned as the men, neither of whom matched their man in the photograph, unloaded about a dozen pieces of artwork into the gallery. They didn't remove anything from the warehouse and were headed back to the van after a few minutes and drove away.

The gallery owner lowered the garage door.

"Hmm." He didn't know what to think. He pushed the lid of the dumpster open and then helped Trinity out before he joined her in the alley.

The "homeless couple" approached them. Charlie waved a hand in front of his face. "The two of you stink."

"Tell me something I don't know," Kyle said quietly. He looked to his team, hoping they had something useful to report.

"While they were distracted," Paige said, "I got their plate number along with a look inside the van through the windshield."

"You discover anything interesting?" Kyle doubted they saw much but held out hope for a lead.

Paige shook her head. "Unfortunately, no. I'll send you the pictures I took. Maybe you'll see something I missed."

"Sounds good. We need to go clean up. I'll meet up

with you later."

"Want us to follow up with the owner?" Charlie asked.

"No. I want to go through those pictures first. Send me what you know about the van owner too." He motioned to Trinity to follow him.

"Where do you think you're going?" Trinity stood with hands at her waist.

"To your car."

"No way. My car will reek. We'll take a bus."

He stifled a groan. "You sure about that? Aren't you afraid people will recognize you from the news?"

"Snap. You're right. Fine. We'll take my car, but keep the windows down. I don't care if it starts to rain again or not."

He nodded. Worked for him. He had no desire to be cooped up with their stench. He drove them back to his place on autopilot as he considered the facts.

"Umm, Kyle?" Trinity sounded uneasy.

"What's up?"

"I just remembered I'm wearing my only clean set of clothes."

"That's a problem." He'd be cutting it close, but they could probably cross the lake, go to her apartment and then swing by his place before Sally showed up for protection duty. He accelerated. "We'll go to your place first."

"Thanks. I'm sure glad he didn't get crazy at my

apartment and destroy my clothes like he did at your place."

"Something tells me he was frustrated when he didn't find what he was looking for at my house."

"Yeah. You're probably right. How did your team know to be at the art gallery?"

His clenched his jaw. Did he tell the truth or make something up? Truth. "We have your phone tapped."

"You what!"

"Now calm down. It was done legally. Based on the information you provided along with some intel, I'm not at liberty to share, we were able to acquire a warrant to listen to your incoming phone calls. Unfortunately, your tipster kept the call too short for us to trace it."

"I suppose I should've expected something like that. This changes everything."

He glanced her way and then focused on the road again. "What do you mean?"

"You betrayed me. How can I trust you now?"

"Trust goes both ways, Trinity. You neglected to tell me about the phone call, remember?"

She frowned. "I explained that."

"Next time, wake me up. Believe it or not, I care about what happens to you. Who knows what could have happened if you'd shown up there alone?"

"I know what wouldn't have happened. I wouldn't stink like rotting food." She stuck her nose out the window.

He grinned but quickly forced a neutral look on his face. If she knew how messy things could get in his line of work, she'd sprint in the opposite direction. He chuckled at the thought.

"You think this is funny?" She snapped.

"No, sorry. I let my mind wander." Somehow he needed to ease the tension between them. But how?

# 7

Trinity slammed the news van's door and strode toward the courthouse where a press conference would be happening momentarily. Sally walked a couple feet in front of her. Her protector looked for trouble.

Cameraman Rick, a twenty-something all around nice guy, followed on Trinity's heels. "What's eating you today? You're not normally so uptight."

She glanced over her shoulder. Rick was more observant than she'd realized. "Sorry. Rough morning." She slowed, allowing him to catch up. "May I ask you a personal question?"

"Okay."

"Do I smell?"

He grinned. "Now that you mention it, you do kind of have a canned tomato thing going on."

She frowned and sniffed the skin on her arm. She had scrubbed and washed her hair twice. Why couldn't she get rid of the odor? "Thanks."

"Don't mention it."

At least Rick could be trusted, unlike Kyle. Her heart hurt from thinking about his betrayal. Tapping her phone without telling her was a violation. But apparently he didn't see it that way. To his way of thinking, and evidently the judge who signed the order, it was for her protection and necessary for their case to listen in on her calls since she had a history of being hostile toward law enforcement. Not true. She was always polite, even when she didn't want to be. She stopped alongside the rest of the press.

Sally stood beside her. "You going to tell me what happened between you and Kyle? The tension rolling off the two of you this morning was thick."

"No. When did you see Kyle?"

"I always check in with him before meeting up with you."

"Why?" Was he pumping her bodyguard for information about her?

"He updates me if there were any problems or new threats to watch for."

"Oh. I see."

"He told me about the dumpster. It sounds awful. Glad I wasn't there."

"Wish I hadn't been. I suppose it's my own fault though, considering I was the one who wanted to stake out the gallery." She probably shouldn't have said that within earshot of a half dozen reporters. Lack of sleep always made her do things she wouldn't do normally.

"Where were you?" Rick asked.

She glanced at her cameraman with his long hair pulled back into a neat ponytail, revealing hollow cheeks and a pointy nose.

She shrugged. "I might as well tell you. While following a lead for a story I'm working on, I found it necessary to hide in a very smelly dumpster."

His light-brown eyes widened. "Thanks for not calling me to assist. Guess that explains the smell."

"Yep." She would take another long shower as soon as she got home tonight. Home. Her own bed sounded wonderful.

"It's really not that bad. Just a hint of an odor," Rick said. "No one will know it's you."

Trinity frowned. Stinking stunk.

The public relations officer stepped up to the podium.

"Looks like we're starting." Trinity pressed play on the voice recorder app and held up her phone. Even though she had the art theft story lead, she still had to cover this for the evening news. Hopefully, doing her job wouldn't keep her away from the smuggling investigation for long.

An hour later, she did a recorded shot on the steps of the courthouse for the evening news. She'd edit when they got back to the station and write up a teaser for the news anchors along with something to post online. Weariness washed over her just thinking about the day ahead. It was a normal day, but she was running on a little more than an hour's sleep.

After work, she'd head back to her apartment. She would not spend another night at Kyle's. The least he could have done was tell her people were listening to her phone conversations—unless he didn't trust her and thought she was in on what was going on. She gasped.

"What's wrong?" Sally stood at alert.

"Sorry. I had a thought that surprised me."

Sally's shoulders eased slightly. "Glad that's all it was."

Surely, she wasn't a suspect in the smuggling ring. No. Kyle might not have filled her in on the details of his investigation, but he wasn't stupid. He knew she was innocent.

They piled into the news van and headed for the station. Rick enjoyed driving, so she let him. At least he was a good driver. She hated navigating the traffic in Seattle. Working in a big city was awesome, but things like traffic were a downfall. Oh well, the price for working in a big market was worth the cost to her way of thinking.

They headed downhill and entered an intersection.

"Look out!" Trinity shouted then everything went black.

Kyle walked casually into Kendall Victoria Gallery. It looked exactly like he expected from the hardwood flooring, to the white walls and paintings that hung along the perimeter. A center wall that divided the front from the back ran horizontally down the middle and also held artwork. The space to his right had several white, waist-high pillars, which displayed glass works as well as pottery. Padded benches were strategically placed throughout the gallery. All in all, the space had a very aesthetically pleasing design.

His phone buzzed. He double-tapped his air pod in his ear. "This is Kyle."

"It's Sally. We had an incident."

Kyle's pulse amped. "Tell me more." He glanced toward Kendall Victoria who approached him, wearing a smile, a chic black dress over her too-thin body.

He returned her smile.

"We were driving back from the courthouse when a truck ran a red light and T-boned us. Our driver never saw it coming."

"Is he okay?"

"I'm afraid not. He died at the scene."

His gut tightened. "How are you and our friend?"

The gallery owner must have realized he was on the phone. Her lips formed an O, and she veered right, close enough to eavesdrop if she was of a mind to.

"Excuse me for one second, Sally." He turned his attention to Kendall. "I just received some bad news. I'll be back later."

Kendall nodded. "I'm so sorry. I hope everything turns out."

"Thanks." He left the gallery. "I'm assuming you're okay since you called. What about Trinity?"

"She's currently in surgery."

He sucked in a breath as tingles shot through him. "Prognosis?" *Lord, please be with Trinity.* How had he grown to care about the woman in such a short time? He wanted to drop everything and go to the hospital, but time was of the essence with the operation, and he couldn't just leave. He had to stop these people to remove the threat against Trinity.

"They wouldn't tell me anything other than to say she's in surgery."

"Okay. I'll talk to her employer and see if they have an emergency contact for her. Any idea if the accident is related to what's going on or if it was a fluke?"

"Not yet. I was told the driver of the other vehicle was cooperating with police. I asked Dillon Brady to see what he can find out for us."

He knew the name and thought for a second. Right. The Seattle cop who frequently helped out Protection Inc. when they found themselves in trouble. He met the officer at Frank's house in December. "Sounds good. If he can't help, I'll look into it." Kyle only needed to make a phone call, but using Dillon was a better idea. The less involved the FBI appeared to be, the better. He didn't know whom to trust—he sounded like Trinity. He frowned. "I'll be in touch. Glad you're okay."

"Thanks. I've updated Frank. I'm going to hang out at the hospital until you get here."

"It won't be until I'm off. I know you need to pick up your daughter. Will you see if Frank can send someone to cover for me?"

"I'll ask. Why can't you come earlier? You can call it work since she's key in your case."

Maybe he could do what he came to do quickly and then head over there if nothing else came up. "I might be able to get over there sooner considering her involvement. At the very least I should interview her to see if she recognized the driver of the other vehicle. See you later." He shot up a prayer for Trinity and the doctor performing her surgery.

He called the news station and was transferred to Trinity's boss before considering the man might not be aware of his other employee's death.

"Clancy speaking."

Too late now. Kyle introduced himself.

"Is this about the accident? The police have already been by since they were in a news van. It's just terrible what happened. A travesty."

"Yes, sir, it is. I'm calling about Trinity. Does she have an emergency contact?"

"Only her dad who's locked up, as I'm sure you already knew."

Kyle rolled his head side to side to ease the building tension in his neck. He was afraid of this. "Is she affiliated with a church?"

"We don't ask those kinds of questions."

"Okay. Is there someone at the station she's friendly with? Someone who might know more about her personal life?"

"She's friendly with Tammy Kline. At least I've

seen the two of them talking."

That didn't sound promising. "Could I get her contact information please?"

Clancy gave it to him without hesitation. "That's her work number. It's against policy to provide her personal number."

"I understand. Maybe you could give her my cell number in case I can't reach her." He rattled off his number to the man and then disconnected the call. He turned and went back inside the gallery. Everything in him wanted to be at the hospital when Trinity came out of surgery, but he could do more good by doing his job. She, of all people, would appreciate that.

Kendall's eyes widened. "You're back. Everything must have worked out."

He shrugged. "A friend of mine told me about this place, and I wanted to see it for myself. I'm new to collecting. Do you have something an entry-level collector might appreciate?"

She nodded. "Of course. Do you have a style you like?"

"Nature photography is my favorite." He looked around the airy space and spotted a wall of black and white photos. "I like color, but I don't see anything like that." His intel stated the artwork on the van this morning was from a suspected art thief out of Spokane. Kendall wouldn't really put stolen art on the gallery walls, would she? He needed to get eyes on the contents of those boxes but didn't have a warrant yet.

Her face brightened. "I might have just the pieces you'd like. I haven't had a chance to see them yet. They came in early this morning from a new-to-us artist over in Spokane. My assistant usually handles artists from that side of the state, but she's under the weather today. Want to take a look?"

"Your assistant?" He already knew to whom she was referring, but he needed to play dumb.

She grinned and offered her hand. "Yes, I'm Kendall, the owner."

He took her hand and gave it a firm shake and then released it. "I'm Kyle. It's nice to meet you."

She dipped her chin. "You too." She scooted past a pillar with a dream catcher hanging from it. "As I said, I haven't had the time to unpack the pieces, but we can go in back and take a look if you'd like."

"That sounds great." He felt as if he'd been handed a lottery ticket. Now to find out if it was a winner.

Kendall's eyes sparkled. "I'm kind of excited to see his work in person. I've only seen pictures online." She chuckled. "Not that it would matter. I've heard his pieces sell so fast they never make it to gallery floors."

"You're kidding. Is that normal?"

"Not in my experience, but we only exhibit Washington State artists here. There are certainly more well-known ones around the world."

Kyle followed her into the backroom where the delivery had been made earlier this morning.

Kendall walked over to what looked to be the same

boxes he'd seen brought in this morning. "Here we go." She carefully opened one box and pulled out a stunning desert landscape with painted accents. She studied it a moment with a puckered brow. "That's odd."

"What's wrong?" He looked at the piece.

"Nothing really. His style is different than I remembered." She turned the piece over and looked at the backside.

"Is everything okay?" Maybe it was a bait and switch scheme.

"Yes." A strained smile covered her face. "What do you think? Is it what you're looking for?"

He looked at the piece and blew out a breath. "I don't know what you were expecting, but that's incredible. I've never seen paint applied to photographs."

"I'm glad you like it. But the quality is not as good as what I saw online." She slipped the piece back into its shipping box. "I'm sure I have something of higher quality that you'll like better. Something worthy of your collection." She motioned toward the door that led to the gallery floor.

"I really liked the one you showed me." He wanted nothing more than to get his hands on the content of those boxes. "I'll pay double the value."

She offered a strained smile. "I can't let you do that. You're a new collector, and I won't take advantage of you like that."

"But I don't mind." He held his breath, hoping the

lure of a big financial payoff would matter to her.

She shook her head. "I'm sorry, but there's something not quite right about it. I can't sell it the way it is."

He frowned. What was going on here? "What about the other boxes. Are those from the same artist? Maybe they're better."

"Perhaps." She opened one more box, pulled out the piece, shook her head, and then angled it toward him. "I'm truly sorry. Perhaps you can come back later after I have a word with Alexis. I think there's been a mix up, and we received the wrong shipment."

"Oh. Okay. Is Alexis your assistant?"

"Yes."

He reached his hands out to hold one. "May I?"

She hesitated then handed it over.

"Thanks." He held it up and peered at the work. It didn't feel too heavy for its size and the framing was perfect. Whoever had done the work was a craftsman. So what was bothering Kendall. "It looks like a masterpiece to me."

Her brow furrowed.

"Did I say something wrong?"

She quickly shook her head and reached for the piece. "No. Sorry. I just realized the time. I need to close the gallery now. I have a lunch appointment."

"Oh. Okay. Well, I can come back."

Her face lit. "Wonderful."

"Maybe I can see the rest then?" He motioned to

the remaining unopened boxes.

"Perhaps." She ushered him to the gallery floor. "Thank you for coming in, Kyle. I hope the next time we meet, I'll have the perfect piece for your collection."

"Well, everything here looks pretty amazing to me. I wish I could buy it all even if it isn't what I had in mind."

She grinned. "I'm sure we'll get something in that you'll like even more. Please be sure to come by often. Our inventory can change at any time."

"I'll do that. I sure wish I could have bought the ones you have in back. How do you find the artists you feature?"

"Most are Washington State-based artists. They can apply online, and sometimes I discover someone's work on my own and invite them to display it here."

"Interesting." He meant it too. She seemed to really love what she did. No wonder she owned a gallery.

She guided him to the door. "I really must lock up."

"Okay. Just one more question. Do you have antiquities or anything like that? I love old art."

She shook her head. "I'm sorry, no. Come back soon."

"Maybe I will. I have a meeting next door. If you're open when it's over I'll pop in."

Worry filled her eyes. "That sounds wonderful. You're in for a treat. Beethoven Café has the best German food. It's quite the experience."

He planted himself in the doorway unwilling to

leave just yet. "What do you recommend there?"

"Honestly, everything is excellent. I eat there a couple times a week. When I opened the gallery Beethoven Café wasn't here yet. I was pretty upset when they first moved in and the fragrance of their food drifted in, but since there was nothing to be done, I figured I'd have to give the place a try. The owner and I are good friends now. Tell Renate hi for me."

It was clear he wouldn't get anything useful out of her right now. What had she seen when she opened those paintings? He stepped out the door. "See you later." He left and called Charlie. "Change in plans. The gallery owner has friends at the German food joint. I don't want anything we say to be overheard by someone there."

"I thought we were going to question the staff about the gallery."

"I will, but I have another job for you because I kind of *have* to go to the café now."

"Uh-oh. What did you do?"

"Nothing. The owner of the gallery is spooked. I need eyes on Kendall Victoria. Is Paige with you."

"I'm here," Paige said. "Want me to tail her? I have her in view."

"Yes. Let me know where she goes and who she talks to."

"On it."

"What about me?" Charlie asked.

"Go with Paige. I'm headed next door for lunch. I

don't want us to be seen together. I also want to see if there's access between the two shops." He ended the call and walked into Beethoven Café right as his phone vibrated, indicating an incoming text from Sally.

*She's out of surgery for a broken arm. Gave doc permission to talk to me. Mild concussion and whiplash. Will be okay.*

Relief surged through him, and his eyes blurred. He blinked away the threat of tears. This reaction was ridiculous. It had to be his lack of sleep the last two nights that caused his emotional response to the good news.

His thumbs moved along the keyboard. *Thanks for the update. Let her know I'm praying for her and will be by this evening.*

A young blonde holding a menu approached him. "Good afternoon. I'm Ashley. Will you be joining us for lunch today?"

"Yes." He slipped his phone into his pocket and quickly scanned the place. Every table along the window was filled with what looked to be people in business meetings. The décor reminded him of the restaurants in Leavenworth—a Bavarian village on the other side of Stephens Pass. He enjoyed visiting the small town occasionally.

Ashley appeared to be in her early twenties. She sported a nose ring and every finger on her hands had some kind of ring on it. "Will anyone be joining you?"

"Not today. This was supposed to be a lunch meeting, but we cancelled last minute. I was next door at the gallery, and Kendall raved about the food here so I decided to come anyway." He walked beside Ashley to a table on the far side of the room.

"Kendall's a regular." She stopped beside a table for two at the far end of the dining room. "Is this okay?"

"It's perfect." He sat and faced the dining area. He couldn't have asked for a better seat as it gave him a full view of the restaurant.

She handed him the menu. "I'll be your server. I highly recommend the spätzle and schnitzel."

"I was told I can't go wrong here, so I'll give it a try." He handed back the menu.

"And to drink?"

"Water and coffee please."

She nodded and shifted to walk away.

"Mind if I ask you a question?"

She shifted back. "Not at all."

"Kendall mentioned that when this place first came in, she was super annoyed by the scent of the food permeating the gallery. I'm trying to figure out how that happens since there should be a firewall between the businesses."

"Oh. That's an easy one." She waved a hand and smiled big. "There's an apartment directly above both businesses. Plus, the kitchen window is almost always open."

How had he not known about the apartment? That should have come up in their research of the building. "Interesting. There's no direct access from one place to the next?"

She frowned. "Not that I've noticed, and I've been here since day one."

"That's impressive. They must like you here."

Her cheeks bloomed pink. "Well, actually, my aunt owns the café. She's the cook too. But it really is a great place to work. I like to visit the gallery on my breaks to sit and take in the art."

"That's convenient." He couldn't quite figure out this young woman. It seemed she had aspirations beyond the café, so why was she still working here. Was it only because of her aunt? "Are you a student?"

"Only of life." She glanced toward the kitchen. "I should go turn in your order."

"Right. Sorry to keep you." If the FBI could get access to that apartment, they would have the perfect place to watch the gallery and their clientele. He'd look into that as soon as he was done here.

A few minutes later, Ashley returned to his table holding a cup of ice water and a coffeepot. She filled his cup. "I asked my aunt about a connecting door. She said our storage room has a door attached to their storage room. Kind of like you see in hotel rooms. She keeps a shelf in front of it so I've never actually seen it."

He nodded. "Thanks for going to the trouble of finding that out for me."

"Sure. I was curious too." She flashed perfect teeth. "Your meal will be out shortly." She hesitated as if she wanted to say more but then walked away.

A plan formed in his mind, and this café could be

key to its success if he could get everything lined up. He glanced toward the kitchen. An older woman watched him from the other side of the pass through. He nodded to her. She frowned and narrowed her eyes. What was up with that?

A moment later, he spotted his meal on the ledge of the pass through. Ashley delivered it. "Enjoy."

"Is that your aunt giving me the stink-eye?"

She sucked in a breath, not even looking in that direction and nodded. "She didn't like you asking questions."

"Oh. I hope I didn't get you into trouble. My mom always told me I ask too many questions."

"It's fine. Enjoy your meal."

He dug into the spätzle first and closed his eyes. The chewy egg noodle was perfection paired with the schnitzel. Too bad he didn't have time to savor the meal.

The café owner wearing a red apron approached him. Her dark hair was pulled up.

He swallowed and steeled himself. She looked ready for battle. She really didn't like questions. Maybe using this place wouldn't work after all.

The woman looked ready to box his ears with her fisted hands. "Do you like?" She stood beside his table and crossed her arms and looked down at him with a furrowed brow.

"Very much. I'm glad you came over. Kendall said to tell you hi. You're Renate, right?"

Her face softened, and she almost smiled. "You're a friend of Kendall's? Why didn't you say so?" She wagged a finger at him. "You just stay away from my niece. She's too young for you."

His jaw dropped. "I agree. You have nothing to worry about with me and your niece."

She nodded once and then marched back to the kitchen.

Talk about awkward. He shoveled the rest of the food into his mouth, left enough money on the table to cover his bill and the tip, and then left while Ashley helped another customer. He didn't want to risk angering the older woman. If his plan was approved, he'd need her cooperation.

Trinity tried to move her head to the side and pain seized her neck. She raised her arm and noted an IV in her hand. She was in the hospital? Then it all came back to her—the box truck had rammed into the driver's side of the news van. No wonder her head pounded. "Hello. Is anyone there?" Had no one come to sit with her? At least her bodyguard should be nearby. But Sally was in the van too. Panic seized her. "Hello!" she called louder.

"I'm here, Trinity." Sally moved to her bedside. "Sorry. I didn't mean to freak you out. I was texting my childcare provider and responded too slow. Do you remember anything about today?"

"The accident but after that, nothing."

"You were awake for a short time and gave the

doctor permission to talk with me. He allowed me to sit with you. By the time I got here, you were zonked."

"I can't remember any of that." How could she forget a conversation with her doctor? "Why don't I remember?"

"I'm sure it's normal. You were recovering from surgery."

"Surgery? What's wrong with me?" Tears burned the backs of her eyes. "Am I paralyzed?"

Sally chuckled. "You have a flare for the dramatic. Can you feel your legs?"

Trinity's face burned. "Now that you mention it, yes. But what about my neck? It really hurts." Come to think of it, so did her right arm. She looked down and grimaced. "What's wrong with my arm?"

"Broken. As for your neck pain, you have whiplash. All things considered, you're a blessed lady."

"What about you? How did you walk away with only a few cuts and bruises?"

"I didn't see the truck coming, so I didn't tense up. I'm guessing where I was sitting protected me too. I'm sore and will probably hurt like crazy for the rest of the week." She shrugged. "I'm blessed too."

"Too? I don't feel so fortunate after seeing how you walked away from the crash." Her stomach knotted at the look of dread that covered Sally's face. "What aren't you telling me?"

Sally rested her hand on Trinity's. "I'm really sorry, but Rick didn't make it. He was killed instantly and didn't suffer."

The monitor beside Trinity beeped rapidly. "His poor family. This is all my fault."

Concern covered Sally's face. "Look at me." Sally bent over and got in her face. "This is not your fault. Now breathe."

Trinity blinked and did as commanded. In. Out.

"That's it. Slow deep breaths. Good job."

The monitor went back to a normal rhythm.

"Thanks, but how can you say it's not my fault?" She had no doubt the accident had been an attempt on her life. "The bad guys had probably hoped to disable our vehicle and then grab me to get whatever they think I have."

Pain filled Sally's eyes. "You have a wild imagination."

"You don't think I'm right?"

"No. I don't. For starters, the driver of the other vehicle never tried to grab you. No one did. Secondly, there's no evidence to support your theory. The accident looks to be an accident."

"Oh. Well, that's good." But she still felt responsible. If she hadn't gone to the press conference, they wouldn't have been in that intersection. Yes, she was doing her job, but still she felt guilty.

"You okay now?" Sally handed her a wad of tissues and pointed to her face.

Trinity touched her cheek and pulled her wet fingers away. She hadn't realized she was crying. She dabbed her tender skin. Oh boy, did it hurt. "I almost hate to ask, but what do I look like?"

"You ever see someone after they lost a fight?"

Trinity winced. "That bad?"

"Maybe a bit worse, but you'll heal." Sally checked her watch.

"You have a hot date?" Trinity teased.

"As a matter of fact, I do."

"Good for you but don't you think you should reschedule? I mean you've been through a lot today."

Sally chuckled. "Sorry, I misled you. It's not that kind of date. I need to pick up my daughter from her sitter."

"Oh. That's not nearly as much fun."

"But a whole lot safer for my heart. I'm focused on Emma and my own well-being right now."

"Did someone break your heart?"

Sally's face darkened as a storm brewed in her eyes.

"I'm sorry. Don't answer that. I shouldn't have asked such a personal question. Blame the concussion."

Sally dipped her chin.

A rap sounded on the hospital door. Sally moved to check it. "It's Kyle." She started to open the door.

"Stop. He can't see me like this." She had to be a wreck.

"You don't have much choice. He's your bodyguard tonight. I can't stay."

Trinity swallowed the lump in her throat. She was being selfish. "Of course. I'm sorry. Let him in."

"I need to talk with him first." Sally slipped out.

Trinity tried to compose herself before facing Kyle. Dread filled her at the look of horror that would likely show in his eyes. She pushed the thought away. She was alive, and that's what was important. Poor Rick didn't make it. She'd have to have flowers sent to his family.

A rap sounded on her door again.

A tingle shot through her. "Come in."

Kyle walked in. He wore a suit. His tie was loosened at the neck, and he looked as handsome as ever even though he had dark circles under his eyes. "Heard you had a rough day."

She looked at him closely for any hint of pity, and there was none. Relief settled on her. "It could've been worse. Want to sit?"

"Thanks." He sat on the only chair in the room. "Sounds like you'll be here for at least tonight for observation."

"Based on how I feel, that doesn't surprise me. You don't have to stay. You look exhausted. I'm sure you could use a full night of sleep."

"As good as that sounds, you're stuck with me. The police were unable to determine definitively if the accident was an accident."

"Oh! But Sally was so sure it was."

"It appears that way, but we still need to be absolutely certain." He pulled the chair in the room closer to her bed and sat.

She reached for the bed control and raised the back slightly to better see him. "How's the driver from the other vehicle?"

"He wasn't seriously injured."

"Don't you think it's odd that Rick was killed and the driver of the other vehicle wasn't? Was he drunk or high?"

"No. The truck was so much bigger than your vehicle. It protected him."

The door whooshed open, and a nurse walked in.

"Hi, Trinity. I'm Mandy. I'll be your nurse this evening."

An alarm sounded from the hallway. Mandy's eyes widened. "Excuse me." She rushed out.

Kyle stood. "I'll be back."

If she could, she would cover her ears to soften the sound of the piercing noise. It sounded like a fire alarm, but if that was the case, wouldn't Mandy have said something? It had to be some other kind of emergency.

Trinity gasped when the door opened again, and the bushy-eyebrow man from the gallery walked in. Panic seized her. "Who are you? Why have you been following me?"

The man held a finger to his mouth. He clicked the door lock into place and walked toward her slowly, a gun in his hand.

Trinity screamed.

# 8

Pounding sounded outside on Trinity's hospital room door.

Bushy-eyebrow man stalked closer to her. "I don't have much time. Where'd you put it?"

"Put what?" If he would tell her what it was, maybe she'd be able to give him what he wanted. She sure didn't want whatever it was. "I don't know what you're talking about."

He gritted his teeth and reached out toward her. "Look, lady. I'm running out of patience. Either you tell me where the code is or you're done."

That sounded like a death threat. "What do you mean done?" Her voice shook as she stared at the gun.

With his free hand, he ran his finger across his neck.

She needed to stay calm and keep her wits about her. "If I have what you want, wouldn't it make more sense for me to live?"

"After all the trouble you've given me, I don't think

so."

"Tell me about the code. What's it for?"

A sinister smile curved his lips. "Do I look stupid? Now where did you hide the code? I've looked through everything you own, and it's not anywhere. My boss says you have it. She wants it back."

Trinity had seen him for the first time at the gallery, maybe his boss was a woman from there. "Who's your boss?" Trinity pressed her lips together, watching the man's reaction carefully.

He squinted his eyes. "I suggest you cooperate. It'll go much easier on you."

"Is your boss behind the accident that killed my cameraman?"

The thug shrugged. "I want the code. Now!"

Her door whooshed open.

The man whirled around.

No! He couldn't shoot, Kyle. Trinity used her left hand to throw a water bottle at the back of his head.

"Hey!" He whirled back around, giving Kyle time to knock the gun free and subdue the man.

Kyle yanked the man's arms behind his back and slapped cuffs on his wrists.

"I didn't do nothin'."

Trinity winced. "Didn't do anything," she corrected him, as if grammar was the worst of her problems. It wasn't, but that phrase annoyed her.

"That's what I said." He narrowed his eyes.

Kyle pushed the man into the seat. "You did plenty.

Including breaking and entering not only Miss Lockhart's apartment, but my house as well. Not to mention the property damage and menacing."

"You can't prove that was me. I wore gloves."

Trinity almost laughed at the man, but she held it together. She couldn't risk making Kyle's job more difficult.

"Hey, smart guy," Kyle said. "What else did you do so you wouldn't get caught?"

The man's bravado faded as his head tilted forward. "I'm not talking. If I do, I'm dead."

Kyle made a call and then guided his prisoner out of the room while telling him his Miranda rights.

A moment later, Mandy scuttled back into her room. "Well, that was exciting. Are you okay?" She checked the machine showing Trinity's vitals.

"I'm shaken, but no worse for the wear." Did having that man in custody mean she was no longer in danger? No, that couldn't be. He said his boss would be angry. So, if he was behind bars, she'd either send someone else after Trinity or try to get that code herself. What was the code for? Maybe a bus locker or a storage locker. Perhaps it's where they stored the stolen goods. Not likely. Her head pounded, and she closed her eyes.

"Special Agent Richards asked me to tell you, he'll be back ASAP and that another bodyguard is on the way. He asked me to stay close until Dillon Brady arrives. I have other patients, but I'll do my best to make sure no one bothers you. We have extra security on the floor right now, so that will help."

Who was Dillon Brady? The name was familiar, but he wasn't listed as one of the bodyguards on the Protection Inc. website. She groaned. There was so much she didn't know.

"What's wrong?" the nurse asked. "Are you hurting?"

"Yes, but that's not why I groaned. It's not important. Thanks for doing what you can. What was the alarm for?"

"Your intruder pulled the fire alarm. Security caught it on surveillance."

"Figures. I'm sorry for being so much trouble."

Mandy waved a dismissive hand. "It's no trouble. I've seen you on the evening news. You never give a hint of the danger you put yourself in. I had no idea you needed a bodyguard. I'm glad I went into nursing instead of broadcasting."

Until recently, she'd never considered the hazards of her job. "Was journalism a career you considered?"

"Not really, but still…" She gently patted Trinity's hand. "Try and get some rest. I'll make sure no one disturbs you."

"Thank you. Wait. Did Agent Richards say who Dillon is?"

"I believe he said he was a cop."

"Okay. Thanks." She smiled until the kind nurse left her room and then stared at the ceiling. There was no way she'd be sleeping anytime soon. A cop? What was Kyle thinking? He knew how she felt about the police. Things must be worse than she realized if he'd brought in a cop to look out for her.

She pushed thoughts of her newest bodyguard out of her mind. There was nothing she could do about him, and she had something more important to worry about. She needed to talk to Kyle. She looked around for her phone but didn't see it anywhere.

A yawn escaped, reminding her about the abrasions on her face and how tired she felt. Maybe she could rest her eyes for a bit before the cop arrived. She'd ask him for help with finding her phone.

A voice startled her awake. Her eyes shot open. A man stood beside her door. "Who are you?"

He pulled the phone away from his ear and spoke softly. "Dillon Brady. Frank with Protection Inc. asked if I could hang out with you for a few hours. I'm sorry for waking you."

"Oh. I expected a cop in uniform. My nurse told me you were coming. How long have you been here?"

He raised a finger then spoke into his phone. "I need to call you back." He pocketed his phone. "A few minutes. I heard about your accident and what's going on with the gallery. How are you doing?"

"Fine." Though he seemed like a nice guy, she had no intention of being friendly with a cop. Her dad would never approve. "I need my phone. I want to tell Kyle something important. Do you see it anywhere?"

He stepped further into the room and looked

around. "I don't see a phone. I'm happy to text Kyle for you."

"You know him?"

"Our paths have crossed. When the team is in over their heads they reach out to me or Kyle for official help." He grinned. "I'm not sure how that started but it seems to be my calling in life to protect and serve the protectors."

She studied the man. Brown eyes, short brown hair, smile lines around his eyes. He had a boyish charm about him that put her at ease. "Check the restroom please. Maybe they put my stuff in there."

He did as she requested. "Found it." He walked out holding a clear plastic bag. He pulled out her phone and handed it to her.

She took it with her left hand and frowned. This wouldn't work at all. "Maybe you should text him after all."

"Sure." He stood beside her bed with his thumbs poised over the screen. "I'm ready."

"The man who broke in here said he wanted a code. He told me he would kill me if I didn't give it to him."

Dillon looked up. "Was he trying to scare you, or do you think he would actually follow through with the threat?" He must have sent the text because he pocketed his phone.

"He wanted to. He was very angry. Guess I've caused him too much trouble."

Dillon nodded. "He's locked up now, and from

what I heard, he's not getting out soon."

"That's the best news I've heard all day."

"What do you know about the code he wanted?"

"Nothing really, other than we found an old dry cleaner's receipt in my coat pocket that wasn't mine." Why was she telling him this? It must be the trauma of her day.

"Interesting. Oh, I sent the text."

Relief filled her. "Thank you. Until I get use of my right arm again, I'm not sure my phone is going to be of much use to me."

"Yeah, they are a challenge when one-handed."

"How long are you helping out at Protection Inc.?"

"Only until Kyle can come back and take over your protection duty."

She grimaced. "I never imagined I'd need protection. Thanks for coming. I know you didn't have to."

He nodded. "I'm familiar with your case. Frank filled me in. Other than the new development with the code, do you know anything else?"

"I take it Kyle isn't sharing information?" Not that she expected the FBI to allow it, but she thought they might since it could be relevant to keeping her safe.

Dillon shook his head. "That'll be the day. Kyle is a by-the-book kind of agent. I don't mean that to sound derogatory, but he keeps his intel close."

"That sounds like him. Do you have any idea how Sally's doing?" Trinity couldn't help being concerned for her bodyguard. Sally had to be feeling the accident by now, and with a baby to care for, she would more than likely be struggling.

Dillon frowned. "She's sore, but that's all I know. I need to give her a call and check on her."

Though he didn't say as much, the man was concerned for Sally. Was there something going on between the two? Sally hadn't mentioned a special someone. She'd seemed as if she wanted to avoid relationships.

Dillon cleared his throat. "I heard about your cameraman. I'm sorry. Were you close?"

Trinity closed her eyes. It was so difficult to accept that Rick was gone.

"You don't have to answer. I know it's been a day."

"No. It's fine. It's hard to process. It's so new. We weren't friends outside of work, but it's still difficult. I hurt for his family. As soon as I get out of here, I'd like to put together some kind of tribute in memory of him. I'm sure I can find some behind-the-scenes footage to post on social media."

"Any word on if the accident was connected to your situation?"

"Not yet. I sure hope it's not. I don't know if I'd survive the guilt."

He nodded. "I imagine I'd feel the same way. Fatal accidents are thoroughly investigated. You should know something one way or the other once the investigation is complete. I heard there was some confusion about the lights and about whether one of the drivers ran a red one. The witnesses contradicted one another. One driver said the news van had a green light, and a pedestrian said the truck had the green light."

"Is that even possible?" She'd thought those things were run by computers and couldn't mess up.

"Technically it could happen if there was a malfunction. The witnesses said the lights changed to flashing red after the accident, which is the failsafe for a glitch. In your case, it very well could have been a malfunction. Honestly, in all my years as a cop, I've never seen it happen."

"Wow. So we both really could have had green lights. That's crazy. Makes me a little nervous to get back on the road."

"I don't know the stats, but I'd say you have a greater chance of getting struck by lightning than street lights malfunctioning in that way."

"Guess I'm extra unlucky." Since she'd followed that tip about the gallery, her life had been turned upside down. What would happen next? She tried to ignore the unease that filled her and squeezed her eyes shut.

# 9

Kyle pushed open the door into Trinity's hospital room.

"Don't move," Dillon said. "Identify yourself."

"It's Kyle." He'd even sent a text, warning the police officer he was on his way up to the room. He liked how cautious Dillon was with Trinity's safety.

"Okay. Come in."

He entered and spotted Dillon putting his gun into a holster. "Let's talk in the hall." He glanced toward Trinity and schooled his face to show no emotion. She'd been through it today. He hurt for her.

Dillon nodded and met him outside the room. "Sorry about that. I had the nurse's schedule, and no one was supposed to be entering the room."

"You didn't get my text?"

Dillon pulled out his phone and sighed. "I guess I did and didn't know it."

"No worries. How's it going? Any trouble?"

"It's been quiet."

"Glad to hear it. Thanks for the message about the code."

"Any developments with that?" Dillon asked.

"Not yet. How's Trinity?"

"Her nurse seems pleased."

"Good. Thanks for watching out for her. I'll take over now."

"Sure thing. See you around." Dillon walked away without looking back.

Though hospitals were not his favorite place to be, Kyle was happy to be here for Trinity. He hurt for her when he considered all she had been through since Sunday night. A lesser person would have wilted under the stress, but she was strong. He liked that about her. Funny how one of the things that drew him to her was also responsible for him not caring much for her before he'd gotten to know her better.

Kyle pushed back into the room and stood beside the bed for a moment. A peaceful look rested on Trinity's face even though she had to be in at least a little pain. He'd spoken with her nurse before relieving Dillon and found out unless something changed, Trinity would be released tomorrow, which opened up a whole new set of issues. Who would care for her? Sally couldn't play nursemaid and be expected to protect her at the same time.

Then again, Trinity only had a broken arm. Maybe she could manage things on her own. He'd been unsuccessful in locating a feasible emergency contact.

Trinity was alone in the world, unless you counted her dad, which he didn't.

"You're back." Trinity shifted to face him. She had to be feeling better. When he'd seen her before, her mobility had been limited. "What do you know?"

"I heard you have a good chance to be released tomorrow."

"Who told you that?" She frowned. "I thought that was private. No one's supposed to give out information like that without my permission."

"I flashed my badge. Frank and I needed to know how to plan your security. After the incident earlier, your nurse was willing to help."

"I guess I understand that."

"Please don't cause trouble, Trinity." The last thing he wanted was to get the nice nurse who'd helped him into trouble.

"I won't." The tension on her face eased slightly. "Any other news?"

"Nothing I can talk about." His hope of getting a surveillance team into the apartment above the gallery was a bust. As it turned out, it was tenant occupied. He'd gone back to the gallery after his lunch, but it had still been closed and stayed closed for the remainder of the day. He knew first hand since he'd staked out the place. His team would re-group and try again tomorrow. If stolen art was being fenced through the gallery, time was of the essence.

"Does that mean you're making progress or that

you don't know anything?" Trinity looked at him with anxiety.

"No comment." He took her badgering him for information as a good sign. She must feel better than she looked.

"Aw. Come on. Give me something. A nibble."

He chuckled. "You're growing on me, Lockhart."

Her eyes widened at the use of her last name. He rather liked her name. It was catching—a great TV name. Though his background check on her revealed it was her birth name and not an assumed one for her job.

"I'm sorry I can't comment either way. I'll let you know when I have something I can talk about."

She grinned and then winced and touched the hand with an IV in it to her lip. "I expect the scoop before everything goes public."

He sighed, wishing he'd never made that agreement. "I know. Like I said, it's your story to tell." He only hoped nothing leaked to the press in the meantime. He trusted his team to stay quiet, but the more people who were brought into this case, the more the risk of a leak grew, which put Trinity in added jeopardy.

"How about you try to sleep some?"

She looked at him intently as though trying to read his mind—not happening.

He'd been trained well to hide his thoughts from showing on his face. Good thing too. He wouldn't want her to know how much he'd grown to care for her. He needed to finish this case and then see where things went. In the meantime, they needed to remain professional.

Her lips tipped up slightly. "What about you? When will you sleep?"

"When this case is closed."

"Not smart but believe it or not, I understand how you feel. Good night." She shifted until she must have found a comfortable position because no sooner had she stopped moving then her face relaxed and her breathing steadied.

The following morning someone touched Kyle's shoulder. He jerked and opened his eyes. Trinity rested peacefully in the hospital bed a few feet away. He shifted, stretched, and focused his attention on her bodyguard. "Good morning, Sally. What time is it?"

"Seven."

He stood. "If she's released today, will you take her to my place? I had someone come by to clean things up. A friend will be over later today with a bed and sofa to replace what was destroyed. I'll text you his photo later so you know he's safe to let inside."

Sally's eyes widened. "You work fast."

"I spent a lot of time in my car yesterday and took care of several things via my phone." He reminded himself to put one foot in front of the other. "If anything changes, you have my number."

Sally nodded. "Stay safe."

"You too." He left.

Trinity tucked her legs to her side and snuggled into Kyle's new basement sofa. Talk about comfortable. If she wasn't careful, she would fall asleep and lose another day. "I should be at work, not here lounging." Trinity frowned.

"You heard the doctor," Sally said. "You're not to work until next week. Your job right now is to let your body heal."

"Yes, mother. I know, but I don't have to like it." Trinity let her eyes close. "I want to help with the case." If only she wasn't so tired.

"I understand." Sally sat on the other end of the couch and groaned.

"You okay?" Trinity's eyes shot open.

Sally looked miserable. "My back is protesting today. I called Frank and asked him to send a replacement for me."

"Oh." Trinity didn't care for the idea of someone else being her bodyguard, but what was she supposed to do when Sally was clearly in pain. "Are you hurting from the accident?" She didn't think her bodyguard had been injured.

"Yeah. I'm sorer than I expected."

"Makes sense considering the severity of the accident. You need to give your body time to recuperate too."

Sally sucked in a sharp breath as if in pain. "I wonder if your host has a heating pad."

"It wouldn't be down here if he does."

A knock on the basement door sounded. Sally stood slowly. She moved to the side of the entrance. "Who is it?"

"Carissa."

Relief covered Sally's face. She flipped the lock and opened the door. "You're back! Thanks for coming. How was your honeymoon?"

"Too short." Carissa winked.

"Come in, and I'll introduce you to Trinity." Sally guided the tall brunette over to the sofa. "Trinity, this is Carissa Jones, one of the owners of Protection Inc. She's here to take over." Sally glanced at Carissa as if to confirm.

Carissa nodded. "It's nice to meet you. I see you had some trouble yesterday."

Trinity raised her broken arm slightly. "You could say that. Thanks for coming. I was worried about Sally overdoing it. She's really hurting today."

Carissa glanced toward Sally with a furrowed brow. "Maybe you should go see a doctor."

"I'll be fine. It's nothing rest, a heating pad, and an anti-inflammatory painkiller can't fix."

"If you're sure. Take it easy, okay?"

"I'll try."

Trinity watched the concern and care Carissa showed toward Sally and knew she'd be in good hands.

Carissa shooed Sally toward the door.

Sally stopped and reversed course. "I need to run

upstairs and see if Kyle has a heating pad before I leave. I think it'll help Trinity."

Carissa shook her head. "I can get it."

"No. It'll only take a minute. Be right back." Sally walked up the stairs.

"Is she always so stubborn?" Trinity asked.

"Pretty much. It's one of the qualities that makes her good at her job."

A couple minutes later, Sally walked back into the apartment holding a heating pad. "Here you go. I'm sure it'll help your muscles relax." She handed it to Trinity. "I don't think I can bend over to plug it in."

"Don't worry about it. I've got it." Carissa plugged in the heating pad and then turned and walked with Sally to the door. "I'll be praying you feel better soon. You can't work in your condition, so take the rest of the week off. Marc and Frank agreed. You have sick leave, so it's not going to cost you."

The creases on Sally's forehead smoothed. "Thank you. That's a relief. I'm sure I'll be up to doing my job by Monday."

"Hey," Trinity said. "Make sure you call Dillon. He seemed more than a little concerned about you last night."

Sally's face warmed. "Really? Okay. Thanks." Sally looked everywhere but at Carissa's raised brows and fled out the door.

Trinity couldn't stop smiling even though it hurt. The look on Sally's face at the mention of Dillon was priceless. Her bodyguard definitely had interest in the cop. It was nice to know even in her injured state, her instincts were right on. There was something about the way Dillon talked about Sally that made her think something more than what met the eyes was going on with them. Sally's response confirmed it.

Carissa pulled a kitchen chair into the living area and sat. "At the risk of sounding unprofessional, what do you know about Dillon and Sally? I've been out of town and missed whatever dynamic you're referring to."

She respected Sally too much to speculate to her boss. "You'll have to ask Sally. I'm not a gossip."

"Aren't you a reporter? Keep to the facts. No embellishments."

Trinity sobered. "Honestly there are no facts. I thought I saw something on Dillon's face last night when I asked him about Sally."

Carissa chuckled. "You were fishing to see if Sally was interested in Dillon." She crossed her arms. "Looks to me like you're a troublemaker."

The troublemaker tag appeared to follow her no matter where she went. To her way of thinking she wasn't a troublemaker, regardless of what everyone else said. "You wouldn't be the first person to accuse me of that. I read people well. Looks like I read the two of them too."

"I wouldn't be too certain," Carissa said. "I've never seen anything more than professionalism between them."

"I suppose I could be wrong. Maybe I misread embarrassment for interest."

"I'm sure that's what it was. Sally has never said a word to me about Dillon."

"You're close?" Trinity didn't get that impression, but she could have read the women wrong.

Carissa stood. "We're not BFFs, but we talk." She moved to the kitchen and rummaged through the cupboards. "There's no coffee anywhere."

"We've been taking it from Kyle's upstairs."

Carissa sighed, pulled out her phone, and shot off a text.

Trinity raised a brow and looked pointedly at her bodyguard's phone.

"Reinforcements." She tucked her phone into her pocket. "My husband will bring coffee supplies. There're only three things you need to know about me. The first and most important is, I take my job very seriously. Secondly, I exist on coffee, and I'm super picky about the taste. Last but not least, I am fiercely protective of those I care about."

Carissa's passion was a little scary, but Trinity had seen all kinds in her line of work and wouldn't let her bodyguard's statement intimidate her whether that was the intent or not. "Got it. Think I'll go lay down in the bedroom." A new mattress had been delivered earlier, and she couldn't wait to try it out.

Carissa nodded.

When she closed the door to her room, Trinity's

phone indicated an incoming call. She checked the caller ID and smiled. "Hey, Kyle. What's up?" At least her broken arm didn't hamper her ability to talk on the phone.

"When you were at the gallery who was running the exhibit?"

"Alexis was the woman's name. She said she was the hostess. I assumed she was the owner. Remember. I told you this." She couldn't understand why she had to repeat herself so many times to Kyle. Maybe he was testing her—probably.

"Are you sure?"

She frowned. "Well no, I assumed. Was I wrong?" That had to be why he was questioning her again.

"I'm sending you a picture of the actual owner right now."

Her phone indicated the text. She steadied the phone between her knees and then touched the screen. A picture popped up. She frowned. "That's not her. The woman at the gallery that night was around my age or younger. The woman in the picture looks like she's in her forties." She looked closer. "Isn't she the one who opened the garage door?"

"Yes. She's the person who accepted the early-morning delivery. I met her later that day when I visited the gallery pretending to be a customer."

"You're sure about this?" If this was truly the owner, Trinity did not see her at the exhibit.

"Positive. Her name is Kendall Victoria. It took

some digging, but I also learned that the assistant was in charge of that exhibit and dealt directly with the artist whose pieces we saw delivered."

"You've been busy." She'd give almost anything to be working alongside him. She glanced at the closed door. Maybe Carissa would cooperate.

"The sooner we wrap up this case, the faster you get your life back."

"And you get your home back." The accident messed up her plan to return to her own place. She was still uneasy about fully trusting him after learning he had her phone tapped, but she couldn't stay angry with him considering he'd spent the night in a chair to make sure no one tried to hurt her. "Is there anything I can do? Any research? Anything at all?" Okay she sounded desperate, but she didn't care. She needed to do something.

"I need you to stay put. I can do my job better, without having to worry about you too."

"You're no fun." She hurt but there had to be something she could do.

He chuckled. "I'll make it up to you. Talk later."

She looked at the phone and grinned. He'd make it up to her. She liked the sound of that.

# 10

"Afternoon." Kyle walked into the gallery and nodded at the woman he presumed to be Alexis. She fit the description Trinity had given him as well as the DMV photo he'd acquired. Charlie and Paige weren't far behind him. They would pose as a wealthy couple, looking to invest in art. He'd had background supporting Charlie's "extracurricular" activities planted on the dark web in case anyone went looking. While they distracted Alexis, he would wander into the backroom and look for those boxes. If the judge saw the delivery they'd witnessed was still on the premises with photographic evidence, she might be more inclined to issue a search warrant. Without that warrant their hands were tied.

"Is there anything I can help you find, sir?" Alexis flashed a dazzling smile.

"I'm in the market for something that speaks to me."

"You've come to the right place. Take your time

and explore. We have a wide variety of pieces. Let me know if you need any help."

"I will. Thanks." He strolled off to the right of the register. On his previous trip, Kendall had led him to the backroom. If he stood close by, he could go undetected from this trajectory.

The door to the store opened again, and his team walked in. He almost laughed at Paige's getup. She looked like a celebrity from her perfect makeup to stylish clothing. She turned, revealing her long hair in a pretty twist at the base of her neck—a change from her normal look of a standard bun.

Charlie's hand rested on Paige's back as they ambled around the gallery. "Excuse me, miss. What can you tell me about this piece?" He looked at a large painting done in an impressionist style.

That was Kyle's cue to sneak into the backroom. He reached for the doorknob and twisted. Relief filled him when he was able to slip into the back without any obstacles such as a locked door to block his way. A locked door would have foiled the entire plan. He could pretend to be looking for the restroom, even though the door was clearly marked "employees only." He didn't break and enter so at least he had that going for him.

He hustled to the area where the boxes had been yesterday and stopped short. Was the art he'd seen from the delivery really gone? It sure looked that way. A few boxes rested against the wall. He headed in that direction.

"What do you think you're doing?" Alexis stood with hands at her waist, looking none too happy with him.

"I was trying to find the restroom."

"We don't have one for the public. You need to leave this room immediately. Customers are not allowed back here. The sign clearly states 'employees only.'"

"Oh. I'm sorry. Your boss took me back here yesterday. I assumed when I didn't see a restroom out front there would be one here."

"I must ask you to leave immediately. The café next door has a public restroom."

"Of course. My apologies." He marched past her.

Charlie stood alongside Paige, facing the sidewall. He glanced over his shoulder with a furrowed brow.

Kyle pretended to ignore him and headed next door to complete his ruse. If by chance Alexis asked about him there, he wanted to make sure they could say he used the restroom. He pulled the door open to the German café and strode inside. The aroma of spices made his stomach growl.

"You're back," Ashley said. "I thought maybe my aunt scared you away."

He grinned. "Nope. Would it be possible for me to use the restroom? The gallery doesn't have one."

She shook her head. "Alexis must be the one working. She's such a snob about their restroom. Ours is only for customers, but I'll make an exception for you since you've been here before."

"Thanks." He grinned and walked into the restroom. He stood at the sink and washed his hands for a full minute. He twisted the faucet knob to turn off the water then dried his hands and walked out.

Ashley stood nearby. She held a box toward him. "I thought you might enjoy a treat. I put a few complimentary coconut macaroons in there for you."

"Thanks, Ashley." He raised the box to her and then noticed writing on the top—a phone number. "Yours?"

She nodded, unapologetically wearing a confident smile.

"Your aunt would have my head."

She rolled her eyes. "What she doesn't know won't hurt her."

It looked like he wouldn't be coming here again. Bummer, he really liked the food, and this place could prove integral to the operation. "Have a good day, Ashley." With nothing more to say, he left. His team stood at the street corner waiting for the light to change. He lengthened his stride to reach them before they moved into the crosswalk. "How'd it go?" He kept his gaze forward and spoke out of the side of his mouth.

"They're getting a new shipment of highly collectable art on Friday. She's going to call when it arrives."

"Well done." Except for the part of keeping Alexis distracted while he investigated.

The light changed, and they moved into the

crosswalk. "What's in the box?" Paige asked.

"Cookies. You're welcome to have them."

She didn't take the box. "Looks to me like they're from an admirer. A woman, I presume?"

"Yes. What gave it away?"

"The flowery handwriting and the heart. See you at the office."

As they stepped onto the sidewalk, he veered to the left, and his team went straight. Paige was too good at her job, at least when it involved his life. Speaking of his life, he needed to check on Trinity again. He hadn't been able to get her out of his mind since her accident.

# 11

A thud sounded above Trinity as she lounged in Kyle's basement apartment. "What was that?"

Carissa held a finger to her lips and pulled her sidearm. "Stay close. I don't want to leave you alone here in case it was a ploy to distract me."

Trinity's eyes widened, and she stood as fast as her still sore body would allow. "It was probably Kyle. He gets home around this time."

"I'm not willing to take the chance, are you? It's your life at stake."

She shook her head. "I guess not when you word it like that." She followed after her bodyguard who'd been restless for much of the day. So much so Carissa offered to do her makeup to try and hide the bruises. She had a talent too. Trinity, could only see the bruises now if she looked hard. Yes, it had hurt some, but it was worth it.

Carissa crept up the stairs one at time.

A cupboard shut hard upstairs.

"I'm going to open the door," Carissa whispered.

"Stay behind me." She turned the knob, pushed the door open, and then poked her head out. She blew out a breath and turned to face Trinity. "It's Kyle." She spun back to the door and knocked.

"Come in," Kyle said.

They entered his space. Trinity gazed at the man she couldn't get out of her head. "Hi. How was your day?"

He pulled a glass from the cupboard and filled it with water. "Pretty good. I meant to check on you throughout the day, Trinity, but time got away from me. How are you feeling? You look better than the last time I saw you."

"Thanks to Carissa's talent with a makeup brush. I'm not feeling great, but I won't complain." Considering Rick had lost his life and she only had a bruises, a broken arm, and a mild concussion, there was no way she'd complain. She'd had flowers sent to his family today expressing her condolences. It wouldn't bring Rick back, but she hoped the flowers would bring a bit of comfort.

Carissa checked her watch. "I'm glad you're home. I'm sick of staring at your boring apartment walls."

He chuckled. "Sorry about that. I've been too busy to decorate."

Trinity shook her head. "I'm happy you didn't decorate. I'd feel even worse if art had been ruined. Speaking of which, are there any new developments with the gallery?"

Kyle ignored her question and looked at Carissa. "This job is certainly no ocean paradise like when we last worked together."

Carissa smiled wistfully. "I miss Oregon. As for an ocean paradise, you're not kidding. You can't even see Lake Union from here."

He chuckled. "The Lincoln City job was a sweet assignment."

"What am I missing?" Trinity looked from her bodyguard to Kyle.

Kyle raised a glass to Carissa. "I believe this is your story to tell."

"Kyle and I met in a coastal Oregon town on a job. We stayed at the estate of a wealthy family for a summer, protecting their granddaughter. Kyle joined our team while we were there, or so we thought. He was actually undercover for the FBI."

"Wow." Maybe Trinity had gone into the wrong business after all. "That sounds like a primo gig."

Carissa nodded. "You'd think."

"Aw. Come on." Kyle poured water into two glasses. "It wasn't all bad. That's where you and Marc fell in love." He handed them each a glass. "How would you ladies like to accompany me to dinner?" He looked pointedly at Carissa. "Before you bite my head off, I have security worked out. Trinity will be as safe as possible."

Carissa shook her head. "I'm glad to hear it, but count me out. I've already been here longer than planned. You sure going out is wise? I know you have security figured out, but there's always an inherent risk when you're in public."

"Trust me. Trinity's safety is very important to me."

Trinity sucked in a quick breath. Did that mean he felt something more for her than simply being her bodyguard, or was this how it worked? Talk about being confused! Trinity looked at Carissa. "What do you think? Should I go?"

Carissa looked carefully at her. "It's your call. Like I pointed out to Kyle, being in a public space comes with risk no matter how prepared you are, but if you need a change in scenery…"

"I really do." She looked to Kyle. "I'm in." Excitement mixed with a dose of fear filled her.

"Be careful." Carissa stood. "See you tomorrow, Trinity." She strode out the front door.

Kyle locked up after her. "You sure you're up to going out without Carissa?"

"I wouldn't want all the trouble you went to going to waste but…" She narrowed her eyes. "You're up to something." If he hadn't invited her bodyguard, she would think he was asking her on a date, but clearly this was something else.

"Maybe." A twinkle lit his eyes. "Or maybe I'm just tired of freezer meals. I'm starving. You ready to go?"

She shrugged. "Well…" she said teasingly. "It's not like I can cook very well with only one arm."

He laughed. "You're right about me being up to

something. We've made progress with that receipt we found in your coat pocket. There's a place on the Wharf I want to check out with you. I think you could assist me with something there."

Her insides leapt. He wanted her help. She hid her delight and played it cool. "Sounds intriguing. Speaking of the receipt, any progress on figuring out what code your prisoner wanted? He was convinced I had it."

Kyle looked away and set down the glass. "To answer your question, yes, but there's something I need to tell you."

Dread filled her. "This doesn't sound good."

"It's not." Regret laced his voice. "I learned as I was leaving work that he passed today."

"What's that supposed to mean?" It sounded like he was saying the bad guy was dead but that was impossible. The man had looked perfectly healthy. Then it hit her. "Murder or suicide?"

"It was declared a suicide."

Her eyes narrowed. "But you're not convinced?"

"I'm not willing to rule out murder. But what concerns me is that now that he's out of the picture, what will happen next? You saw two men talking, and it looks like there's a woman in charge of this ring. We don't know how many people are involved."

"You think someone else will come after me?"

He nodded.

"And you want to go to the Wharf?" Sure, he said he had security in place, but it sounded risky to her.

"Do you trust me?"

"No. Not after you had my phone tapped, but I'll concede this. You do seem trustworthy when it comes to having my best interest. You appear to want to keep me safe which I greatly appreciate." Time stood still as their gazes held. Her heart raced. His eyes definitely spoke to her, but what were they saying?

"We could both use a little adventure. Don't you think?"

She blinked. "Isn't your entire life an adventure?" She took her now empty water glass to the sink.

"Cute. Some might say so, but this will be fun."

A flitter of pleasure bubbled up inside her. "Okay. I'm in. What should I wear?"

"You're fine as is. It's not fancy."

"Where are we going?"

"It's a surprise, but I hope you like fish." He pulled his jacket from the back of a chair.

"I love fish, and I also love Fisherman's Wharf." She hadn't been there in forever, and she felt much better this evening than earlier, so she planned to enjoy the outing.

Trinity stood inside the bustling seafood restaurant with Kyle beside her. "Look, Sally and Dillon are here." Sally and Dillon were dressed casually in jeans and T-shirts. They looked very comfortable together. Either they were really good friends, or something was going on between them.

"Right on time too."

"They're my security?" She glanced at him. "But Sally can hardly move."

"Which is why I invited Dillon along too." He waved to the duo at the table. "I figured you'd be more comfortable if Sally was here also. Come on. Let's sit."

She'd have preferred a meal alone with him, but it warmed her from head to toe to know he had thought this through.

Kyle pulled out a chair for her at a table situated along the back wall. She sat facing the wall. Then he sat across from her. "Thanks for coming. There's a reason I brought Trinity to this particular restaurant. I'd like to run something by all of you." Kyle looked at Trinity. "Do you mind?"

"Get on with it already. I'm dying of curiosity." Okay, an exaggeration but Trinity really was anxious to know what they were doing here.

A waitress approached with menus and glasses of ice water.

Trinity quickly glanced at the menu. "I'd like the halibut fish and chips please."

"Same for me," Kyle said and handed the sheet of paper back to the waitress.

"Me too," Dillon and Sally said in unison.

A sparkle lit Sally's eyes. She handed the menu to their waitress who nodded and walked away.

"What do you want to run by us?" Dillon asked.

From his inside jacket pocket, Kyle pulled an

evidence bag that held the dry-cleaning receipt. "When we first found this, I thought the dry cleaners was the key, but upon further investigation, we've determined they have nothing to do with the art traffickers, other than this." He pulled a small flashlight from his pocket, but when he switched it on, it was a black light. He flipped the evidence bag over, revealing the backside of the receipt. A series of letters appeared with different letters beneath them along with the name of the restaurant and a riddle.

Trinity gasped. "It's a cipher."

Sally grinned. "Cool, but it's odd that the restaurant name is in different ink and writing."

Kyle shook his head. "Once we figured out the riddle, we added the restaurant name ourselves."

"Oh," Trinity said. "I wondered about that."

Kyle slipped everything back into his pockets "Assuming we figured out the riddle correctly, somewhere in this room is the document we need."

The waitress returned with their meals. "Enjoy. If you need anything else, let me know." She walked away.

Trinity dove into her meal, and Kyle followed suit. Her appetite had finally returned, and she was starving. She glanced at Sally who must not be as hungry as the rest of them based on the fact she was looking around the restaurant rather than eating.

Sally reached for a fry. "I'm guessing what we need is in plain sight. Something that's always here." Her gaze landed on the menus on the hostess stand. "Be right back." She stood and retrieved one from the hostess then brought it back to the table.

"The menu?" Dillon stopped eating. "Great idea."

"Thanks. Now to see if it works." Sally handed the single sheet of paper to Kyle who quickly pushed his food aside and studied the words. "Got it."

Trinity swallowed. "So fast? Is cryptology one of your hidden talents?"

"Actually, yes. But this is a basic monoalphabetic cipher." He turned the receipt around. See how each letter is assigned a substitution? To be honest, a child could have figured it out once they knew where to look. According to the next clue we need to take a whirl on the Great Wheel to find the next clue."

"I've always wanted to ride that." Trinity took a big bite of her last fish stick then covered her mouth afraid something might fall out. Not the best way to make a good impression on Kyle.

Sally chuckled. "You in a hurry?"

Trinity took a gulp from her water. "When you're in my business, you learn to eat fast. You never know when you'll have to rush to the site of breaking news."

Kyle downed his fish sticks in a few bites too.

Sally's eyes widened. "And what's your excuse?"

Kyle reached for his water glass. "I haven't eaten since breakfast. Besides, the sooner we leave, the quicker we can solve this—"

"The sooner Trinity gets her life back," Dillon finished.

"I was thinking, the sooner we wrap up this operation, but you're not wrong." Kyle flashed a roguish grin at Trinity.

Trinity's face heated. If she didn't know better, she'd think he was implying something deeper. Even though she was attracted to the man, they were an impossible fit. Like two pieces of a puzzle that never quite matched. He was the good guy, and she was the daughter of a bad guy. Which disqualified her to be with a man like him, considering the FBI rejected her.

Kyle paid for all their tickets to ride the wheel, and then they all boarded the same gondola. He and Trinity sat on one bench and Dillon and Sally sat across from them. The wheel moved, and they climbed higher. "The clue says 'from the wheel the arrow marks the spot.'" As they rose higher, he searched the city skyline.

"There!" Trinity pointed to a billboard with an arrow.

He fist-bumped her. "Way to go. I believe you're right. We have two more trips around. Keep looking." He continued to scan the skyline. So far, tonight had gone off without a hitch, and they were one step closer to figuring out the code. He and his team had taken great precautions. Besides Dillon and Sally, Charlie and Paige had been seated nearby, keeping an eye out for trouble at the restaurant. Right now, his team kept watch on the ground and would alert him if anything looked out of the ordinary.

Dillon sat tall and leaned forward. "I wonder…"

"What?" Sally asked.

"See the cranes at the shipping yard. Don't they resemble arrows?" Dillon waved his finger in the air presumably outlining the large contraptions. "You have to use your imagination a bit, but an argument could be made that those are arrows."

Kyle nodded. "It's a risky location. The art could easily come and go in shipping containers, but why take the risk of the authorities discovering it? There are much safer ways to smuggle merchandise."

"Unless the art is coming from another country," Trinity said. "I heard a story about a tourist who had purchased what she thought was a copy of a masterpiece. She'd had it shipped back to the States, and then customs confiscated it and accused her of stealing the original. As it turned out it really was the original. To say she was surprised is an understatement."

Kyle nodded. "I suppose it's possible. We should at least check out the shipping yards. I'll also talk to a source I have there. He might have heard something." The gondola came to a stop. The door opened. "We're leaving." He got out first and stood beside the door.

"I thought we had more time." Trinity followed between Dillon and Sally.

"Technically you're correct. But this wasn't a pleasure ride."

Trinity looked toward the operator and then at him.

"I see your friend. The one who came to your apartment when it was ransacked."

"You're observant." He couldn't help smiling. He really liked how Trinity's mind was always working.

Glass shattered. He ducked and pulled Trinity down with him. Concrete kicked up. "Shots fired! Get down!"

# 12

"Move!" Kyle shouted over the chaos as tourists scattered in every direction.

Sally and Dillon used their bodies to shield Trinity as they stayed low and rushed behind a nearby building for protection.

"Anyone notice which direction those came from?" he asked.

"East," Dillon said.

Kyle scanned the area across the way for the shooter who was likely long gone. Charlie and Paige ran toward them crouched.

Charlie stopped beside him. "Everyone okay here?"

"I think so." He looked at Trinity, whose face had paled. "You okay?"

"Yes."

"How about the two of you?" he asked Sally and Dillon.

"I'm fine," Sally said.

"Same." Dillon shifted to the right. "I saw the

shooter on the balcony of that building."

"On it." Charlie pulled out his phone.

Police sirens blared.

"Paige and I will deal with the local police," Charlie said.

"Perfect." He quickly filled in his team on what they'd come up with. "When you're done here, head to the shipping yard terminal. I'll work on a warrant."

"You have your hands full," Paige said. "I can get the warrant while Charlie deals with this. We don't both need to be here."

"That works too. I'll be in touch." He turned to Trinity and spoke into her ear. "Let's get out of here while we still can. Whoever shot at us is likely on the move." He wrapped his hand around her good arm and gently guided her toward his vehicle as quickly as she seemed able. He sure didn't want her to end up back in the hospital because she pushed herself too hard.

Sally strode at Trinity's right with her head on a swivel. She kept an eye on their surroundings like the pro she was. "We'll follow in Dillon's car."

"I'm sending my team to the shipping terminals to look for anything suspicious." His top priority right now was Trinity's safety.

"What about the billboard arrow?" Trinity asked.

Frustration filled him. He couldn't be everywhere at once. Assistant Special Agent Gibson was a good man but he could be difficult to work for. He needed more feet on the ground, but ASAC Gibson would only give him Charlie and Paige. Kyle blew out a breath. "I'll come back and follow that lead after you're in a secure place."

"Seriously?" she practically shouted. "You're not leaving me."

"What do you suggest?" he asked, working hard to tamp his aggravation.

"I go wherever you go."

"Impossible. In case you forgot, you were in a serious car accident. And you were just shot at. As far as I'm concerned you're a walking miracle. I know you're tough, but even you must have your limits."

"I'm fine."

He glanced her way. "I'm sorry, Trinity. This is the way it has to be."

Pain etched on her face, and her shoulders drooped ever so slightly. She was not fine and probably only felt that way because of adrenaline. Once it wore off, she'd crash.

"This rots." Determination rested on her face as he opened the passenger door to his vehicle. She slid in as he rushed around to the driver's side and Sally watched on.

"You ready?" He started the engine.

"Always," Trinity said.

"I meant are you buckled?"

"Yes. Now go." Urgency filled Trinity's voice. "I have a bad feeling. We need to get away from here."

He pulled into traffic with a look in his rear-view

mirror. Sally was hurrying toward Dillon's vehicle.

Kyle needed a safe place to take Trinity. Frank would have an idea. Using Bluetooth he placed the call.

"Kyle, how's it going?" Frank's voice had a cheerful lilt. At least one of them was having a good evening.

"We took fire tonight. I need a safe place for Trinity."

"Bring her to my house. I had state-of-the-art security installed. There's no way anyone's breaking down my front door again."

Kyle thought back to the week of Christmas when someone had done exactly that to his door. Granted it had taken a small explosive to do so. "We're on our way."

"We'll be ready and waiting."

Kyle ended the call. How had the shooter known they would be at Fisherman's Wharf? Had they been followed? No, he would've noticed. Maybe one of the others had been followed. It couldn't have been Charlie or Paige. They were too good at their jobs, but Sally wasn't used to fieldwork like this.

"He said 'we.' Who's we?" Trinity asked.

"I'm guessing he'll call in backup. You've only met the women of Protection Inc., but there are also a couple of men—Carissa's husband, Marc, and Peter. I've known Marc since our days as military police. I'd trust him with my life."

"Good to know. What about Peter?"

"I don't know him well, but Frank trusts him, and

that's good enough for me."

"Wow. That's a lot of faith to put in someone."

"It's deserved." He and Frank had gone through a few rough patches since they'd met, but they'd come to an understanding. He trusted Frank probably more than he should, but integrity was practically the man's middle name.

"Didn't you say he was a former cop?"

He glanced at Trinity.

She sat stiffly in the passenger seat with her jaw jutted forward.

"He is. You have to trust your team, Trinity. We are all doing our best to keep you alive."

"I know, but I can't help wondering how the shooter knew I'd be at the Wharf tonight when I didn't even know."

"That's been bugging me too. All I can think of is Sally or Dillon were followed. They're known to have been protecting you, so it stands to reason someone would be watching them on the chance one of them would lead the shooter to you."

"That sounds reasonable. I shouldn't blame Frank then?"

"No, you shouldn't. I neglected to tell him about my plans for this evening and that I talked Sally into joining us off the books, same with Dillon."

"Wow. These people are saints." She shook her head. "They barely know me. Why would they do that?"

"It's who they are. Dillon is one of the best cops I

know, and you're aware of what I think of the Protection Inc. team. Frank is the best person to keep you safe right now. I need to get back to my team and follow up on the clues as well as see if anyone found the shooter." As much as he wanted to take care of Trinity himself, other than Marc, there was no one he trusted as much as Frank with the woman who had captivated him since she'd broken into his home.

"Okay. I'm convinced. If I'm honest, which I will be, I trust you more than anyone I've ever known. I don't trust easy, and it was touch and go when you tapped my phone, but I've had time to think about that. I forgive you. You've proven yourself to me. If you say Frank will protect me then that's good enough."

"Why?" he asked. She'd said something similar before, and he hadn't followed up on it, but he really wanted to know what made him different.

"Why? Isn't it enough to know I trust you?" Confusion filled her voice.

"No. Well, yes, but why do you trust me more than anyone you've known? You have to have had someone else you trusted as much as me at some point in your life."

"Not really. It was just me and my dad growing up and well, we both know how dumb trusting him would have been."

"No teacher? A best friend? A youth pastor? What about your mom?"

She laughed. "Me in church while living with my

dad? You've got to be kidding. He was a thief. Remember? Stepping into church would have been incredibly hypocritical. Don't you think?"

"Depends. If he gave up his life of crime and confessed, it wouldn't be hypocritical at all."

"Yeah, well, that never happened." She barked a laugh. "My dad wouldn't even drive down a block if there was a church on it."

"Wow. That's some serious avoidance. Any idea why other than the law-breaking thing?"

"He said the church failed him and his family, and he wanted nothing to do with it. Plus my mom was a Christian. She left him when she discovered he was a thief. At least that's what he told me. I don't remember her."

"She left you with him?"

"Don't go there, Kyle. You do not want to open that Pandora's box right now."

"Got it. My faith in God is paramount in my life. Though I don't always make it to church. What about you?"

"Do I have faith in God? Yes. I do. I consider myself a Christian. Though I don't think it's the same kind of thing you have going on. Do I attend church? No."

"Because of your dad?" It made sense, considering she didn't like cops because of the man's influence. That she had faith in God was almost shocking when her dad's influence was taken into account.

"Mostly because of him. I'll deny it if you repeat this, but churches scare me."

Sadness and remorse filled him for what her childhood must have been like. "Why? I mean other than your dad's influence."

"This might be my dad's influence since I've only walked inside a church building a handful of times, but I feel like I wouldn't measure up. Like I'd make some unforgivable faux pas or do something to make people dislike me. It's a lot of pressure."

He wanted to tell her that was crazy but knew it wouldn't be helpful. They were almost to Frank's. *Lord I could use some wisdom here.* "First off, you don't have to go to a church to be disliked or make a faux pas."

She laughed. "True. But still. I really care what people think about me. It would hurt to disappoint them."

His hands tightened on the steering wheel. "There is no way you will ever be able to please everyone, so get that out of your head right now."

"I know, but it's hard. I know I have a reputation among law enforcement that's not flattering so this might be hard to believe, but I'm a people pleaser. I want people to like me."

"Cops aren't people?"

"Of course they are, but they're not high on my list of people I want to impress."

Her dad had really done a number on her, but she'd come around and accepted Protection Inc. and even

Dillon who was a legit cop, so there had to be hope for her. "Okay. But remember, we are all imperfect humans who should strive to be the best we are able to be with our Heavenly Father's help. We can't do it on our own. Being around other Christians helps you grow in your faith."

She tilted her head to the side and appeared to be thinking. "I never thought about it that way. I found a church online that I like. It's actually in the greater Seattle area. Maybe someday I'll work up the courage to check it out in person."

"That would be pretty cool. Let me know, and I'll go with you."

"For real?"

He winced at the surprise in her voice. Clearly, she didn't understand how much he liked her. Sure, she annoyed him, and he razzed her, but that didn't change how he felt. "Absolutely. One more thing you should keep in mind is, not everyone who attends a church is a Christian. No church is perfect and no person is perfect. Give yourself some grace to make mistakes."

He saw her nod out of the corner of his eye as he pulled into the driveway of Frank's two-story house. "We're here."

Dillon and Sally parked along the curb.

Trinity released her seatbelt. "Good talk. I'll think about what you said while I'm hiding out here. How long will I have to stay?"

He got out and quickly moved to her side of the vehicle.

Dillon and Sally approached him.

He looked around for anyone suspicious. He'd been certain no one followed them besides the duo. The only other person around was a man walking his dog, so Kyle opened the door. "Let's get you inside. As for how long you'll be here, I don't know. I'll be in touch."

The door swung open before he could ring the bell. Frank motioned them inside.

Kyle shook Frank's hand. "Thanks. I can't stay. I'll be in touch as soon as I'm able."

Frank nodded then focused on Trinity. "How about you fill me in on your evening."

She looked at Kyle.

"It's fine to tell him. Thanks again, Frank." He nodded to Sally and Dillon before rushing back to his vehicle. He prayed they'd wrap up this operation tonight.

Trinity studied the man Kyle had abandoned her with. He had dark hair with a little gray around the temples. He looked strong, like he lifted weights. Overall, he appeared to be fit.

A woman with long dishwater blonde hair walked into the entryway from what appeared to be the kitchen. She smiled. "Hi, I'm Katrina. Frank's girlfriend. I pulled a cherry pie from the oven a little while ago. Would you like a piece?" Katrina's eyes sparkled.

Trinity sniffed the air. How had she not noticed the scent of cooked cherries? "Sure. That's nice. Thank you." She really wasn't a fan of cherry pie but didn't want to be rude to this couple protecting her.

"Follow me, everyone. Dessert awaits." Katrina turned and headed straight ahead through a doorway to the kitchen. A hall that led to what appeared to be the family room was to the right beside a staircase. "Have a seat at the bar. I'll cut us each a slice."

"Better make it seven," Frank said. "Carissa and Marc are on their way. They should be here soon."

Trinity looked from Frank to Katrina. "Are you a bodyguard too, Katrina?" Kyle hadn't mentioned her.

"Goodness, no. I was here baking when Kyle called. Frank asked me to stick around until Carissa and Marc arrived, but since Sally and Dillon are here, I'll head out as soon as we have pie."

"But why leave?" Trinity couldn't see any good reason for the woman to be kicked out.

"I was sort of a client of Protection Inc. once, and to be honest, I don't have the stomach for danger."

Frank sat beside Trinity as his gaze rested on Katrina. "You're welcome to stay nonetheless."

Katrina slid two plates each with a piece of pie over to them. "You don't need me here to distract you." She smiled with love-filled eyes at Frank.

"You win." Frank forked a bite of pie into his mouth.

Sally declined pie. "We'll head out as soon as the others get here. My sitter turns into a pumpkin soon."

"I'm her ride, so I'll be heading out too," Dillon

said.

Frank's chewing slowed as he looked from Sally to Dillon. "I'm sure there's a story here, but we'll have to save it for another time."

Sally shook her head. "No story, just logistics."

*Snap.* Trinity really thought those two had chemistry. Too bad neither of them was aware. She took a small bite and was pleasantly surprised. "This is actually good, Katrina. I'm not a cherry pie person, but I like yours."

Frank grinned as he forked another bite. "She's quite the baker."

The doorbell peeled.

Frank stood. "Be right back." A moment later, he reentered the kitchen with Marc and Carissa on his heels.

"Long time, no see," Carissa said to Trinity.

"Yeah. Sorry about that. I'm sure you're sick of me." She hated to cause Carissa more work when she should be having a romantic night with her man.

Carissa shook her head. "Not yet." She sniffed the air. "That pie smells delicious."

Katrina handed her a plate. "I started coffee. I used the beans you gave us."

Trinity chuckled. "You have a reputation, Carissa. I mean, I knew you were serious about coffee, but this is next level."

Marc rolled his eyes. "You have no idea." He held out his left hand. "We haven't officially met. You were in the bedroom when I dropped by Kyle's to deliver coffee."

She took his hand with her good arm. It sure felt weird shaking hands with the wrong hand. "It's nice to meet you. I'm sorry for dragging you over here."

He waved off her concern. "This is what we do."

Sally and Dillon headed for the door and slipped out unceremoniously.

Trinity had a feeling these people must be incredibly close. Their rapport was like that of a tight-knit family.

Katrina slipped into her jacket. "Good night, everyone."

"I'll walk you home." Frank wiped his mouth on a napkin and stood. "Be right back." A moment later, they were gone.

Trinity turned to Carissa. "What am I missing? He's walking her home? She didn't drive?" Though come to think of it, she hadn't noticed a car out front.

"She lives across the street. I'm sure you've heard of her since you're a reporter. Do you recall a house explosion the week of Christmas?"

Trinity's eyes widened. "That was Katrina's house?" She had no idea since she hadn't been assigned to the story and hadn't taken the effort to pay attention to the coverage. She generally buried herself in books during the holidays to avoid all the festivities. They weren't much fun without a family to celebrate with.

Marc picked up a plate with an untouched piece of

pie. "That was a very interesting week to say the least." He looked toward the front door. "I kind of thought those two would be engaged by now."

Carissa shook her head. "You of all people should know better. He's not one to rush into marriage."

There had to be more to this story. Trinity opened her mouth to ask as the front door swung open. "It's me," Frank said. He strode into the family room. "Now that we're all here, how about filling us in on what went down tonight?"

Carissa handed Trinity a cup of coffee. "You look like you need this."

"Thanks." She joined the others in the family room, sat on a leather pouf, and filled them in on the events of the evening.

Marc leaned forward. He wore a puzzled look and rested his elbows on his knees.

"What are you thinking, Marc?" Frank asked.

"We know the unidentified subjects believe Trinity has a code they need. We know the FBI cracked the code. What we don't know is why they would shoot at them without knowing what the code said since they clearly need it. Why try to kill the people with the information they need?"

Trinity shook her head. "Maybe they weren't trying to kill me. Maybe it was a warning. The man who broke into my hospital room said if I didn't give him the code, I was dead. I know he was working for someone, so maybe they had someone send me a message."

Carissa rested her coffee mug on her leg. "Or they were trying to take out Kyle. He's FBI, and they know it. He's in their way since he keeps stopping them from getting to Trinity."

Frank nodded. "You could be right."

Marc stood, pulling his phone from his jean's pocket. "I need to warn Kyle." He walked into another part of the house.

Unease grew in Trinity's stomach. She had dragged all of these people into danger. But wasn't this what they'd signed up for as bodyguards? She refused to allow guilt to overwhelm her. The only thing she'd done wrong was to get caught spying on those men in the backroom of the gallery.

Frank clicked on the television and flipped to the station she worked for. Tammy Kline, her closest friend at the news station, stood before the screen. "It appears the shooting this evening at the Great Wheel was random. Thankfully, no one was injured. Back to you in the studio."

Frank muted the sound. "Did she sound disappointed, or was that my imagination."

Trinity almost spewed the coffee in her mouth. He was right. Tammy had seemed disappointed. The reporter had a flair for the dramatic and enjoyed reporting on shocking events. "She was also wrong. There was no way that shooting was random."

# 13

Kyle pulled up to Frank's house at one in the morning. All the lights were off. Maybe coming back here had been a bad idea. If someone was targeting him like Marc suggested, he could be endangering Trinity. Yet his gut told him Marc was off base. Sure those bullets had struck as close to him as they had to Trinity since she'd been by his side, but that didn't mean he was the target. In fact, he suspected they were only warnings, and the shooter had no intention of hitting either of them.

He yawned. Frank was expecting him. He got out and approached the door, which opened before he got to it.

Frank, looking no worse for the wear, stood in sweats and a T-shirt. "'Bout time you got here."

Kyle stepped inside. "Tell me about it. Tonight was a wild goose chase. If that code was supposed to lead someone to something, I don't know what they were looking for. We found nothing out of the ordinary."

"Maybe that's the problem. Perhaps what you need to find is hidden in plain sight."

"It's possible. But I don't know what I'm looking for." He followed Frank to the family room. "Where is everyone?"

"Sleeping upstairs."

"What's sleep?" Slumber had eluded him for days now. If he didn't get a solid four to six hours soon, he would be in trouble. He yawned again.

"How about you crash on the couch for a few hours? I'll wake you at five, and we'll talk strategy."

"I can't sleep. Too much is at stake. The operation. Trinity. My job."

"Your job is on the line?" Concern covered Frank's face.

"Let's just say failure is not an option." He'd had to do a lot of talking to convince his ASAC to let him pursue this operation.

Frank sighed. "I don't know why you do it."

"'Cause I love it like you love what you do. There are days I question my sanity, but I'm doing what I want to do."

"Give yourself a little time to rest. I find I think best when I'm trying to sleep. Trinity is safe here, and you're in no condition to drive. I'll wake you at five if you fall asleep."

"Maybe you're right. A nap might be exactly what I need to wrap my brain around our next move. See you at five." He kicked off his shoes and rested his head back on the soft throw pillow.

When he'd returned to the waterfront earlier, he'd met up with Charlie across the street from the scene of the shooting. Together they'd searched the area where the billboard arrow had pointed and found nothing worth noting. When Paige had secured the search warrant, they had met up at one of the four shipyard terminals but found nothing. He had hoped the need to search all four wouldn't be necessary, but that had been a dream. What were they missing? Were they even on the right path?

An idea percolated, but he couldn't do anything about it until the gallery opened tomorrow. He would be there when the doors opened.

Trinity sat at the kitchen bar in Frank's house. She'd slept fitfully, but still felt rested, which was nice after the past few days.

Sally walked in, holding a box of donuts in one arm and her daughter in the other. "Did someone order donuts?"

Sally must be the team's cheerleader. It seemed to come natural to her to look for ways to boost morale. "Trinity, this is Emma."

"It's a pleasure to meet you, Emma."

The little girl grinned.

"Did I hear someone say donuts?" Carissa's face brightened upon entering and seeing Emma. "Look who's here," she said with love in her voice.

"Miss Rissa." Emma held out her arms to Carissa.

Carissa relieved Sally of Emma. "Thanks for bringing donuts. You know, this Miss Rissa thing has to stop."

Sally frowned. "I can't figure it out either. She generally doesn't struggle saying words."

Carissa seemed in deep thought. "Frank used to call me CJ until I convinced him not to. I suppose if it's easier…"

Sally shook her head. "No way. If that's not a name you like, she shouldn't use it."

Carissa playfully poked Emma's belly. "She's so adorable I can deal with whatever she calls me for now at least."

Sally opened the donut box. "I feel like I missed out on a slumber party. Please tell me everyone slept."

Carissa reached for a donut with her free hand. "I think so. I was up before the sun and came down to start coffee. Kyle was snoring."

"Was not." Kyle moved to sit on a barstool.

"Was too," Carissa mouthed to Sally. "He's a little crabby today. Glad you brought donuts."

Frank and Marc walked into the room and each took a donut.

"Who are you calling crabby?" Kyle asked.

Sally chuckled and set the donuts on the counter. "Enjoy. I can't stay long. I need to get Miss Emma to her sitter."

"I wish she could hang out with us." Carissa tickled Emma's belly.

Emma rewarded her with a belly laugh.

Marc grinned, looking lovingly at his wife. "We need to make this quick. I have a client's home I need to get to and so does Frank. Carissa will be with Trinity today."

"What about me?" Sally asked. "I feel good enough to work."

"You're on medical leave." Frank grabbed a maple bar. "I was surprised to get your call this morning."

"After last night, I figured I'd be needed."

"We can always use more eyes and ears," Carissa said. "But let your body heal. We'll have you back to work and wishing for a vacation on Monday."

"But I like to keep busy." Sally's happy face faded. She looked beyond disappointed to be excluded from the team.

Trinity felt bad for her. After all, it was because of her she'd been hurt and subsequently put on medical leave. "Aren't we just hanging out here today, Carissa?"

"Yes."

"So what would it hurt to let Sally hang out with us?"

"Tell you what," Frank said. "I'll call if anything comes up and we need you. In the meantime, take a day for yourself."

Sally looked at her boss. "Promise you'll call?"

"You have my word."

"Okay. What's new with Trinity's case?" She reached for a glazed donut.

Kyle cleared his throat. "We didn't find anything last night. Before I send my team back to the shipping yards, I'm going to try another tactic. I hate to waste man hours following a useless lead."

"What's your new tactic?" Marc asked.

"The gallery owner." He brought his coffee mug to his lips.

Everyone focused on Kyle.

"What?" Kyle placed the mug on the counter and looked at all of them with a furrowed brow.

Frank shook his head. "You left us hanging. What's your plan?"

Kyle shook his head. "That's need-to-know."

A collective sigh filled the room.

Sally chuckled. "Guess we know where we stand." She reached her arms out to Carissa for her daughter. "Don't forget to call me if you need anything."

Trinity walked Sally to the door. "I'm sorry about how last night turned out."

"You have nothing to be sorry for. I knew there was a risk something could happen. That's why I was there. To keep you safe."

"Thank you. You might have been there to keep me safe, but your presence was the calming force I needed. Being shot at rattled me."

"You're a reporter. I thought they had nerves of steel."

"Being shot at will rattle the best of us."

Sally grinned. "I was teasing." She lowered her

voice and glanced toward the kitchen. "Don't tell anyone, but being shot at rattles me too, just not in the moment. That comes later."

For some reason this surprised Trinity. She imagined a former cop turned bodyguard had no fear. "Makes sense. Well, I should get back in there before one of them comes looking for me."

"Right. Step away from the door. You shouldn't be exposed."

Trinity moved to the side and then locked the door after Sally left. She walked back to the kitchen and poured a cup of coffee. From what she'd heard, today would be a mind-numbingly boring day. It would've been fun to have Sally here, but she understood why Frank insisted she rest. They needed her healthy.

Kyle caught her eye. He stood and moved toward her. "A word?"

She followed him to the door.

"I can't tell you any details, but if things go as I hope, you'll have your story and I'll have wrapped up this operation."

"Really? I thought last night was a bust." She kept her voice low.

"It was and it wasn't. I'm not at liberty to say more." His eyes sought hers. "When this is over, we need to talk." He lightly touched her cheek with the back of his hand.

She tipped her face toward his warmth before she realized what she was doing. "I'd like that." But was it a good idea? Her heart said yes, but her mind said no.

He moved his hand away slowly.

She let out the breath she'd been holding. "Be careful."

"Always."

She locked up after him and turned to see Carissa standing in the doorway to the kitchen.

"How much of that did you hear?"

A smug smile rested on Carissa's face. "Enough to know our FBI friend is smitten."

"I don't know about that." But she hoped Carissa was right. She needed to do some soul searching today and figure out exactly what she wanted. Right now, her feelings were so mixed up she didn't know how to proceed.

# 14

Kyle strode into the gallery. He had the okay to put his plan into action. He hoped and prayed it would work. Trinity's life depended on it.

Kendall looked up from a laptop. Her face brightened when she spotted him. "You're back." She strolled toward him. "We acquired a new piece I think you'll love."

"Really? I can't wait to see it." He glanced around the gallery. "I stopped by yesterday, but you weren't here, and your assistant wasn't helpful."

Kendall's brow furrowed. "I'm sorry to hear that. Between you and me, I'm beginning to wonder about her. Alexis has an exceptional resumé, but perhaps it's too exceptional if you know what I mean."

"You think she padded it?" Why would Kendall tell him this?

Kendall nodded. Her cheeks bloomed pink. "I shouldn't have said that. Please forgive my lack of professionalism."

"There's nothing to forgive. I hope you feel free to say anything you'd like to me." Maybe she had stumbled onto what her assistant had been doing, or maybe Alexis simply wasn't living up to her expectations. Either way, he planned to use the situation to his advantage.

"There's something about you that makes me feel like I can talk freely with you. Renate said you came by her place the other day. What did you think of the food?"

"Delicious." It looked like his lunch next door had done more than he'd anticipated. He enjoyed surprises like this.

"I told you." Kendall grinned. "Anyway, about that piece. I set it aside for you when I saw it this morning."

"Did you receive several new pieces?"

"Only the one piece. It's from an artist in Tacoma. She's up and coming, and I believe she'll one day be quite collectable."

He rubbed his hands together. "I can't wait to see."

Kendall smiled. "Follow me."

He followed her to the counter where she had been working on her laptop. He had thoroughly vetted Kendall and planned to bring her in on what was going on right in front of her, but he needed to get her away from here to talk privately. "I noticed a coffee shop on the corner. Is it any good?"

"I like it." She reached down and picked up a small canvas holding the painted side away from him.

"Want to join me for a cup of coffee there?" Even

though the gallery was empty, he didn't want to be interrupted by incoming customers or be possibly overheard if someone had planted listening devices in the space.

Her lips parted and her eyes widened. "I um… sure."

"We could go now." He really didn't care about the art and had only used it to have a legitimate reason to be here. If it was a piece the FBI was interested in, there was no way Kendall would have it.

She looked around the gallery. Foot traffic was nonexistent. Even the sidewalks were on the quieter side today. "That works, but first…" She flipped the eight by ten inch canvas around revealing an ocean side photo of children playing in the sand. "It's an original and one of a kind."

"It's a photograph, or wait…" He looked closer. There were brush strokes but it was so vivid and realistic it looked like a photo. "It's remarkable. How did she do that?"

"She's talented."

He really hadn't planned to buy anything, but wow. "How much?"

"For you, one hundred dollars. Don't tell anyone I gave you such a steal."

"Won't the artist have a problem with that?" It had to be worth twice that at the very least.

She shook her head. "I cut out my commission."

"But why?"

"As soon as I saw this, I thought of you. I didn't want money to keep you from it."

"You thought of me?" He must have made more of an impression than he'd realized. Did she think he was poor? He looked down at his worn shoes. Well, maybe he did give off a low budget kind of vibe. "Thank you. Consider it sold." He pulled out his wallet.

She took his money and placed it in the register. "Of course I can't guarantee it, but I suspect you'll more than double your money in the not-too-distant future."

"I don't plan to sell it." It would look nice in Trinity's beach-themed apartment.

Kendall grinned. "I knew you'd love it." She wrapped the piece in craft paper then walked around the counter and handed it to him. "You ready?"

He nodded, suddenly wondering if bringing her in on his case was a wise decision. No, he couldn't allow her kindness to him to stop him from doing his job. They needed her cooperation to take down this art theft ring.

Kendall flipped the sign to "closed" and put a note on the door that said the time she would be back. "Thanks for asking me to coffee."

"Sure. There's something I want to discuss with you."

Her face lit in curiosity. "Oh?"

"Yes. It's related to your business."

"I see." Disappointment laced her tone. "What about it?"

"Let's get our drinks. Then we'll talk." He pulled open the door to the coffee shop. Upbeat music played but not too loud. The rich scent of coffee greeted him. No one stood in line. "What would you like?"

She looked at the cashier. "Small hot raspberry mocha please."

"That sounds good. I'll have the same." He paid, and then they waited on their order.

"I'm intrigued by your reason for asking me to coffee." Kendall's brow puckered.

The barista handed them their drinks.

They headed to two brown leather club chairs across the room and sat.

Kendall angled the chair slightly and then sat and crossed her legs. "So what's this about?"

He pulled out his badge and tilted it for her eyes only. No one else was in the shop, but he didn't want anyone working there to see it. "Someone at your gallery is suspected of using your store to fence stolen art."

She gasped. "That's…" Her shoulders sagged and her brain seemed to stall, but she recovered quickly. "Highly possible. But you must know I'm not involved since you came to me."

He nodded, hiding his own surprise that she knew or at least suspected what was going on. Why hadn't she contacted the authorities? "We believe Alexis is the mastermind, and we need your help."

She blew out a breath. "I wish I could say I'm

shocked at what she's doing. When you were at my gallery earlier in the week, and I pulled out the pieces from Spokane I realized something was off with it, which is why I wouldn't let you purchase it." She looked down and ran her hand around her coffee cup. "I wasn't completely honest with you that day. The craftsmanship on the pieces was exquisite, but I spotted a print behind it. Whoever had put it together had been sloppy, at least to my trained eye."

"Are you saying that a stolen piece of art was set behind the one you showed me?"

She nodded and looked up and off to the side. "The thing is, I didn't know what was going on. You have to believe me."

"Of course. I thoroughly vetted you before bringing you into my confidence. What else can you tell me?" Unease nibbled at him. Something wasn't right here, but he couldn't place what. Everything he had learned about Kendall suggested she was on the up and up and telling the truth, but why wouldn't she look at him? She must feel bad about turning a blind eye to her employee's crimes.

"That day you were at the gallery, I couldn't be sure of anything. I needed to look into the matter, but by the time I returned to the gallery, the pieces were gone."

"What did you do about it? Did you confront Alexis?"

"She said she already had a buyer who had come in while I was out." She shrugged. "I was so surprised, I let it drop."

"I see." He took a sip of the mocha, trying to appear casual when he felt anything but. Kendall knew something, even if she didn't realize what she knew. He didn't want to do something to spook her. "Do you remember anything about the hidden painting?"

"No. I never had the opportunity to look. Like I said, all the boxes that had come in that morning were gone. Alexis took them. She doesn't know it, but I have security cameras all over the gallery, including the backroom. For the record, your little adventure yesterday is on it."

He cleared his throat. "I was looking for the restroom."

"So I heard, but we both know that's not entirely true. You were hoping for a look at those pieces again. Am I right?" She raised a well-manicured brow.

"Yes. But I didn't touch anything." Unease tickled the back of his mind. Was Kendall playing him? He needed to tread carefully.

"I know. I also heard you went next door and used their restroom, so even though you looked to be snooping I half-believe your story about looking for the restroom."

"They seriously told you?" Sure, he had gone there on purpose in case Alexis had been suspicious and inquired but it had been out of extreme caution. He hadn't actually thought anyone would check up on him. Well, apparently Alexis hadn't, but Kendall had.

"Yes of course. Renate is a good friend. I've been

so stressed. I went to meet with my attorney the last time I saw you at the gallery, which is why I was in a rush to leave."

That matched up with what Paige had noted when she'd followed Kendall. "I see. But you had only just noticed the pieces. How was it you already had an appointment?"

Her brow puckered. "There have been other little things that have caused me concern with Alexis. I wanted to meet with him to find out if I could fire her without risking a lawsuit."

"Did you report your suspicion to the authorities after meeting with your attorney?" He hadn't seen anything indicating she had, but maybe he had missed it.

She sipped her coffee. "No. I thought if I didn't say anything that maybe Alexis would leave without causing me any trouble."

"You fired her?" That would complicate things if she had.

"Not yet. I planned to do so this afternoon."

He leaned forward. "Please don't do that. She's working with some dangerous people. People who have ransacked two apartments and shot at me and my colleagues to find something they believe a woman took from the Sunday evening exhibit."

Kendall's jaw slackened. "You're kidding! Oh my. I had no idea how serious this was. What do they want?"

He studied her face, still uneasy about her involvement and lack of forthcoming with the police.

"I'm sorry. I can't reveal that."

"I understand, but…" She pulled an envelope from her purse and slid it over to him.

"What's this?"

"I found it on the floor in the backroom Sunday afternoon."

He looked at the paper. Another cipher and code! This one was not written in special ink. Why was the code on the back of the receipt he'd found in Trinity's pocket written in invisible ink and this one wasn't? It didn't add up, unless they decided the invisible code was too easy to lose.

"You're quiet," Kendall said.

"I'm thinking. May I keep this?"

"Sure."

He tucked it into his inside jacket pocket. "Have you ever found anything like this before?"

She shook her head. "I considered tossing it until I noticed Alexis searching for something in the backroom. I didn't know what she was looking for, but this was the only thing that made sense even if the words on the page were nonsensical."

He'd easily decoded the note intended for Alexis. It didn't seem all that important unless it was a code within a code. "Does the gallery ever get shipments from other countries?"

"Not officially. As you know we only display Pacific Northwest artists, mostly from Washington."

"What do you mean not officially?"

"Well, when I travel overseas, I'll have pieces shipped here. I travel abroad a couple times a year."

He recalled seeing in his background search that she'd been to Europe last month. "When did you last travel?"

"Last month actually. I love the Christmas markets in Germany and France."

"Did you ship anything home?" So far everything she said matched his intel. Maybe his unease was for nothing.

She hesitated. "Why are you asking? How do my shopping habits relate to your investigation?"

He reached for his coffee. "I'm just curious. I have a bad habit of being nosy. I've always wanted to take a few months and tour Europe."

"I imagine that's difficult with the kind of job you have. She cradled her coffee cup between her hands. "Mind if I offer you a bit of advice?"

"Go ahead." This ought to be interesting.

"Life is too short to put off traveling." She raised a shoulder. "At least that's my motto. I try and live each day to the fullest. If traveling Europe is something you want to do, then you need to plan a trip. Dreams need action to be fulfilled."

He nodded. "Advice received." Kendall didn't strike him as the adventurous sort. Driven would be a better word. "Does anyone besides your attorney know you're onto Alexis? Did you tell Renate by chance?"

She shook her head. "I didn't want to drag her into my problems. She has enough of her own without me adding to her load."

"Okay. I'll be in touch. Please try to act normal, and whatever you do, don't fire Alexis."

"I won't. It's not like she's stealing from me." She nibbled distractedly on her bottom lip.

"What's wrong?" There were so many things she could be worried about he didn't dare assume.

She looked up at him blankly.

"I asked what's wrong? You seem worried."

"I am. If the media gets wind of what's going on, my reputation will be ruined. No one will want to put their art in my gallery."

He sucked in a breath. He hadn't considered the ramifications of their operation to her future livelihood. "I suppose that's something you'll have to be prepared for." If she had gone to the authorities to begin with, she could have controlled the story with the media. As it stood now, anything could happen.

"I should get back to the gallery. I don't like to be gone for long." She stood. "When will I see you again?"

"I don't know, but I'll be in touch." He looked toward the window facing the sidewalk where Charlie stood pretending to be a homeless person again while keeping an eye on the gallery for suspicious activity.

The pieces to this case were falling into place. Now all they needed was for everything to go off without a hitch. The thing that bothered him the most was the code. It didn't appear to be of real importance, yet someone was willing to kill for it. What they missing?

# 15

Trinity paced Frank's family room while Carissa spoke on the phone in the front room. How long would they expect her to stay put here? She felt much better today and sitting around doing nothing was driving her nuts. She needed to work whether her doctor approved or not.

Carissa strolled into the room and stopped short. "Uh-oh. You're up to something."

"Not unless you count losing my mind from boredom and plotting a way to get back to work today being up to something." Why had she told Carissa that? She'd only try and stop her.

"That counts. I was told you weren't cleared to return to work until Monday."

"That's technically correct, but seriously, I feel good enough." She'd keep to herself how sore her neck was and that she could use a strong painkiller to take the edge off her arm pain. But she refused to take anything stronger than ibuprofen.

"I can appreciate your situation, but it's not wise to push yourself. Like I told Sally, take advantage of the time off. I'm sure you don't get it often."

"That's for sure, but I don't like having time off. I enjoy my job, and I need to be productive. Can we at least go pick up my laptop from the station?"

Carissa crossed her arms. "Why?"

"I'm sure I have e-mails to respond to." Having her laptop wasn't really all that important. She could access everything from her phone, though it was slow going with one hand out of commission. She wanted to be in the newsroom again, to feel the energy, and more importantly to feel normal again.

"You really expect me to believe you want me to drive you all the way to the news station, risk being followed by whomever shot at you last night, all so you can check e-mails? Nope. Not happening." Carissa nodded toward Trinity's smartphone that sat beside her on the cushion. "If e-mails are really your concern, log into them from your phone."

"Fine. I will." She reached for her phone and then stopped and sighed. "I miss the action. I need to get back to work. I'm going nuts sitting around here with nothing to do."

"Look, I get it, but this is the safest place you can be until the FBI makes more arrests. I know it's not fun being in someone else's home, but let's try to make the best of it."

"How?" She appreciated her bodyguard's positive

vibe, but it wasn't helping.

"We could watch a movie, play a game, deep clean the house, bake, find recipes online and make a nice meal, crochet, knit, or sew."

Trinity laughed at the last few suggestions. "Do you carry yarn with you?"

"As a matter of fact I do. Knitting is a new hobby. I can get my stuff from the car if you'd like to learn."

She was serious. Trinity had thought Carissa was messing with her. "No, thanks. But maybe cooking would be fun." Plus, it would be an excuse to get out of here to pick up supplies.

"Cool. I'll see what we have on hand. Then we'll find a recipe that will work."

Trinity sighed. So much for getting out of here. "It's too bad Kyle and his team couldn't figure out the significance of the clues in the code."

"Yeah. What did it say?"

"I don't recall the exact words, but it said to ride the Great Wheel and look for the arrow."

"The arrow?" Carissa tilted her head to the side. "I wonder if that was figurative or literal."

"We thought it was literal. A billboard had an arrow on it. Then Dillon thought the cranes down at the shipping years looked kind of like arrows too."

"It almost sounds like the code is part of a greater plan. I wonder if it's a game of sorts."

"People don't kill over games." Trinity shook her head.

"They do if the stakes are high enough."

Trinity couldn't accept that the clues in the code were a simple game. They had to mean something more, but what? "I can't see that. What if the arrows pointed to a meeting spot? Maybe they figured out the FBI was onto them."

Carissa shook her head. "Maybe that's why they were so desperate to get it back. But keep in mind the code was dropped in your pocket to figure out before you involved Kyle."

"Right. I forgot. This has been a long week."

"It's been eventful. I'm sure Kyle and his team have things handled. Don't wear yourself out trying to figure out the purpose of the code. For all we know, they could be eccentric criminals who enjoy the thrill of the adventure. If you ask me, the only reason no one can figure this out is because we're missing key information."

"Like what?" Trinity asked.

"We don't know the purpose of the code. We've made assumptions, but if we're wrong, then the code doesn't make sense."

"So you think our assumption that the arrows point to stolen property is wrong?"

"I do." Carissa seemed confident in her opinion.

Trinity didn't know what to think. All she knew for sure was that she wanted her life back.

The doorbell rang.

A jolt of fear zipped through Trinity. She needed to

get a grip. A simple doorbell ring should not make her afraid.

Carissa touched a finger to her lips and pulled her gun. "Stay out of sight." She walked to the door. "May I help you?"

"I have a delivery for Trinity Lockhart that needs to be signed for."

"I can sign."

"It must be signed by Trinity," the man said.

"Are you trying to tell me who I am?" Her voice rose.

"No, ma'am. Please sign here."

"Thank you." The door closed. Carissa walked back into the room, holding a package about the size of a box of ice cream in one hand and her phone in the other. She took a picture and sent it to someone.

"Who's it from?" Trinity stood and walked toward Carissa.

"More importantly, who knows you're here?" Her phone rang. "Thoughts?"

Trinity heard Frank's voice on the other end. She heard the word bomb and began to shake. Was a bomb in the package? Had they progressed from wanting the code to wanting her dead? She hadn't done anything.

"Okay. I'll let you know what happens." Carissa pocketed her phone and rushed toward the door that led to the garage.

"What are you doing? What about the box?"

"Frank has a containment box in the garage." A

moment later, Carissa returned. "The bomb squad will be here in a little while."

"Are we safe?" Trinity's pulse raced. "We need to leave before it goes off!" She stood. They really believed a bomb was in the box. When would this end?

She allowed Carissa to guide her back onto the sofa. How could the woman be so calm? Wasn't she afraid to die? For that matter, wasn't it her job to keep Trinity alive?

Carissa sat beside her. "We're safe. Frank said the box would contain an explosion if there's a bomb inside. If there's not an explosive device in the package, the bomb squad will figure that out."

Trinity crossed her arms and glared at Carissa. "I realize Frank's word is gold with all of you, but it's not with me. I want out of here now."

"You're not a prisoner, but I strongly recommend you stay put. Whoever sent it could be trying to flush us out to get to you."

"But why?" Trinity couldn't help the frustration in her voice. "Why kill me? I don't know anything. I don't have anything."

A loud pop sounded in the garage. Carissa raced to the door and yanked it open.

Trinity followed and looked past her to the smoking box. "It really did have a bomb!" Her body shook, and her legs turned to rubber. She sank to the laundry room floor and leaned against the wall for support.

Carissa's hand rested on her shoulder. "The good

news is you're alive."

"What's the bad news?"

"Someone really wants you dead. I wasn't convinced until now. We need to figure out why. I don't think it's related to the gallery."

Trinity looked up at Carissa. "Why not? That's when all my trouble started."

Carissa offered her a hand to help her up.

"Thanks." Trinity walked back to the couch thankful it wasn't far, considering how wobbly her legs still felt.

Carissa sat in the chair Frank normally used. "What do you know or have that's worth killing for?"

Her mind blanked. This couldn't be real. She had to be having a nightmare. She pinched her leg. Nope. She was wide awake. She took a cleansing breath and tried to focus. Had she overheard a conversation or seen something she shouldn't have? She closed her eyes and dug deep. She opened her eyes and met Carissa's gaze. "I can think of absolutely nothing, but that doesn't mean they don't believe otherwise."

"I hear you, but humor me. Is there anyone out for revenge? Have any of your stories destroyed someone or given them cause to blame you for their trouble?"

"Of course. I do stories like that all the time."

"I thought you were a crime reporter."

"I am, but I also investigate consumer complaints to get to the bottom of situations. I've helped a lot of people find justice." She draped her good arm across her middle and rested her broken arm on top of it, hugging herself. "There are more than a handful of people in law enforcement who don't like me, but not enough to kill me." At least she hoped not.

"You sure about that? Even I've heard a few rumblings about how your reporting has caused some trouble for those in law enforcement."

Trinity spared her a scathing glance. If she caused trouble for cops, it was their own fault. She'd not done anything worth killing for.

"You've caused hardship to others. Maybe someone snapped." Carissa seemed to be talking to herself more than Trinity. "How do I access all your stories?"

"They're online."

Carissa pulled out her phone.

"Go to the station's site then search my name."

Carissa blew out a long breath. "This is going to take a while. You should look too and see if anything catches your attention. Something that seemed innocuous might look different now after all that's happened."

The doorbell rang. A loud voice boomed. "King County Sheriff Bomb Squad."

Carissa hustled to the door. "It already blew. It's in a containment box in the garage. I'll open the door for you." She raced back and pressed the automatic garage door opener. "Stay inside, Trinity. I'll be back to help with the story search as soon as I can."

Trinity scrolled through her phone trying to

concentrate but really wanted to be in the garage where the action was. How long would Carissa be out there? It had been at least thirty minutes since the bomb squad had arrived. She closed her eyes. *Lord, please help me.* She opened her eyes and jumped when the garage door swung open. "Kyle?"

"I came as soon as I heard." He rushed toward her.

Her heart pumped wildly at the passion in his eyes. "I'm glad you're here."

He sat close to her and cradled her good hand between his. "You have no idea how scared I was when I heard the news."

"How did you know?"

"Frank." He looked her over from head to toe. "You're okay?"

"Yes. Carissa knew what to do."

He released her hand and turned all business. "We need to talk. Tell me everything that happened." He pressed *record* on his phone.

Without leaving any details out, including the conversation she had overheard between Carissa and the delivery person, she filled him in on her conversation with Carissa and about her search.

"I need to talk to that delivery driver."

"You think he was in on it?"

Kyle shook his head. "Not likely, considering he was willing to keep the package if he didn't get you to sign for it. Carissa saved the man's life with her wit and quick thinking."

"She saved our lives too. That containment box is impressive."

He nodded. "I think I agree with Carissa's hypothesis. Whoever sent that bomb is likely not related to the gallery. Smuggling stolen art and sending bombs is a huge leap."

"I'm going along with her theory, but I have a hard time believing they aren't related. It's too coincidental."

"Maybe. Maybe not. You've been in the news lately and not on the reporting side. You've become the story, and someone may have decided to use that to their advantage."

"I was in a car accident. That's it."

"In a news van where the driver was killed. Like it or not, your accident has been a top story. Your station has covered it with new developments every evening since the accident."

Trinity sighed. She hadn't been watching the news, which showed how crazy her week had been. News was her life, and she generally followed the headlines. This week she didn't know any. "What do I do?"

His face softened. He reached for her hand and gave it a light squeeze. "Hang in there. The art fencing operation is about to be blown wide open."

She winced.

"Sorry. Poor choice in words."

"You think?" she teased tiredly.

"Hang tight. I need to take care of a few things." He went into the garage.

A text message from her work phone number forwarded to her personal phone. She had set it up to forward months ago after getting tired of carrying around two phones. She read the message.

*You got lucky this time. Next time you won't.*

She didn't read the rest of the message before racing to the garage door. She pulled it open. "Carissa! Kyle! I need you."

Carissa jerked her head in Trinity's direction, and she hustled over. "What's wrong?"

Kyle strode toward her without asking any questions.

She handed Kyle the phone with the message still showing, and he held it out for all of them to see. "'You got lucky. Next time you won't. I trusted you to help, but you only made things worse. Don't bother with your FBI friend. He can't help you. He's in bed with the enemy.'"

Trinity gasped.

Kyle looked up with furrowed brows. "I'm in bed with the enemy? What is this person talking about?" Confusion filled his voice.

Trinity shook her head. "I hadn't read past the first two sentences. What changed today? This came from my informant. The one who contacted me about the gallery."

"So you really don't know the person?" he asked.

She resisted rolling her eyes. How many times did she have to tell him? "If I did, I'd tell you."

"I need to see the security footage Frank has for his entrance. We need to find that delivery person to see if he knows who hired him."

"Whoever he works for, it's a small business. I didn't recognize the company name on his jacket." Carissa charged toward the stairs. "Frank's computer is in his office upstairs. Be right back."

"The bomb was set on a timer, rigged to go off at noon," Kyle said.

Trinity gasped. "But it blew up within five minutes of getting here. If the driver had been any later…" Clearly her informant didn't care who got hurt.

Carissa raced back into the room holding a laptop. "That surprised me too. I figured we had more time. I'm sure glad Frank had that containment box here."

"Why does he have one of those?" Trinity asked.

Carissa's fingers moved across the keys. Within a minute she had the man's face on the screen. "Protection Inc. owns two. One is stored at the office. The other is here—he's a little paranoid after what happened to Katrina's house."

Kyle snapped a picture with his phone. "Excuse me. I need to make a call." He walked to the front room.

"Who do you think he's calling?" She asked Carissa and lowered her voice. "Do you think it's the person he's supposed to be in bed with?" She couldn't help wondering if there was any truth to the informant's assertion.

"There is no way he's on the wrong side of the law." Carissa paused and frowned. "At least not on purpose. I suspect he's working on finding that driver and then dealing with whomever he's supposedly in bed with. How reliable is your source?"

"He hasn't been wrong yet." Trinity concentrated on breathing and forced down panic that threatened to overwhelm her.

Worry filled Carissa's eyes. "If, and that's a big if, your informant's right then Kyle trusted the wrong person. He's one of the good guys."

"You don't think he's dirty then?" Relief coursed through her.

"Absolutely not, but he might have trusted the wrong person."

Cold fear raced through Trinity. Kyle was the smartest person she knew. If he trusted the wrong person, was there hope for anyone? How could she trust her own instincts if Kyle got it wrong?

Carissa touched her shoulder. "Hey, what's going on? You look lost."

"I've been fooling myself. I don't know if Kyle told you or not, but I have trust issues—especially when it comes to cops. Without going into the why, just know that me trusting you and your team of former police officers was nothing short of a miracle, but I trusted you because Kyle did, and I trust him more than anyone ever."

"Wow. Why? It's not that he's not worthy of that,

but he's human. We all make mistakes. There is only One you can trust like that."

Trinity tilted her head to the side. "Who are you talking about?"

"The Lord. God the Father and Jesus."

"That's more than one," Trinity teased. She wasn't completely ignorant about God. "I didn't realize you're a Christian."

"I'm a newish one. God and Jesus are both referred to as Lord. Jesus is God's son, but they are also referred to as being one."

"That's not confusing," Trinity said sarcastically and then decided to give Carissa a break. "I'm messing with you. I really do understand. I watch a church online that I like. I've noticed that the name Lord is used synonymously for God and Jesus.

Carissa grinned. "Good. Then you know you can trust Them."

"Yes, but to be honest, I never thought about trusting God like that." Hadn't she done exactly that when she'd prayed a bit ago? Maybe she was putting trust in Him without realizing it.

"You should. He will never lie to you or lead you astray. He loves you and wants the best for you. You can trust that even if nothing else makes sense. That being said, I don't always agree with what He thinks is best, but in the end, I've always realized He knew more than I did, and He was right."

Trinity shook her head. "That's a huge leap of faith.

I'm not sure I can do that."

Carissa's face brightened. "Think of it this way. Your editor tells you to change a word, but you don't want to. You do it anyway because you have an obligation to listen to your editor. Later, you find out the word you planned to use meant something completely different than you realized, and your editor saved you a lot of grief."

Now that made a lot of sense. "So you're saying God is like the editor of our lives."

"Yes, but you can choose to listen or not."

Trinity nodded. "I know you said you're a Christian, but you talk like you have a real relationship with God. Like He's a real person. How is that possible?" She found the preaching interesting and challenging at times during the services she watched, but generally didn't think about them once she logged off her computer. It sounded like Carissa made her religion her life.

"Do you own a Bible?"

Trinity thought for a second. "I don't think so." How had she not thought to buy one?

"Hold on." Carissa walked into the kitchen and pulled open a drawer. She pulled out a tiny book, small enough to fit into her coat pocket. "This is a New Testament Bible. I'll bookmark something you should read. It'll explain everything."

Trinity watched Carissa flip through until she got to a page that said John at the top. She pulled a gum wrapper from her pocket, ripped it into two pieces then slipped it into the page. "I'm marking John chapter three and Luke chapters twenty-three and twenty-four. I think it'll help you understand why you can trust the Lord and why He wants the best for you." She handed the Bible to Trinity. "Keep it. Frank buys them in bulk to give away."

"You're kidding." Frank was an interesting man.

"Nope. He's the reason I'm a Christian."

"Huh." She held the Bible in her left hand. "Thanks. Guess I have something to do now since I'm stuck here and cooking is out." This was the last thing she expected to be doing today, but she really wanted to know what those passages said, assuming she could wrap her brain around it in her state of distress.

Carissa grinned. "It was part of my grand plan all along." She winked and then headed toward the front of the house where Kyle had gone.

Trinity curled her legs to the side and leaned against the arm of the couch resting the unopened Bible in her hand. Someone had tried to kill her! Someone was watching the house and knew she was here! Why did her informant want her dead?

# 16

The base of Kyle's head throbbed as he paced the front room in Frank's house. He couldn't get that text message out of his mind. Assuming Trinity's informant was telling the truth, he'd made a huge mistake. Who had he trusted? The only person he could think of was Kendall. The unease he'd felt while talking to her came to mind, but he'd attributed it to his overly cautious nature. Nothing had come up to indicate Kendall was part of the ring fencing stolen art. Had they missed something? Was she in on it with Alexis? If so, trusting her and revealing the FBI's involvement put their entire operation in jeopardy.

He called Charlie and Paige, getting them all on the line together. He filled them in on the latest. "It's too risky to wait to act. I say we take them down today before they have time to disappear."

"I'll get the warrants," Paige said.

"We're supposed to meet with Alexis this afternoon sometime," Charlie said. "I'm waiting on the call for an exact time."

"You still watching the gallery?" Kyle asked.

"Affirmative. I'm beginning to wonder about the café next door."

"How so?"

"A male in his thirties walked in there about ten minutes ago carrying a box that would easily fit a canvas," Charlie said.

"Hmm. Did he come from the gallery?"

"Negative. It's a gut feeling something is up," Charlie said.

"Okay. I'll get someone inside the café. Stand by." Kyle shot off a text and then returned to his conversation. "Done. Now let's come up with a plan for how we're going to take down this ring." He hated that they had to move so quickly and risk missing key players, but if Kendall was involved, they needed to act fast.

Thirty minutes later, he pocketed his phone and then headed back to the family room where Trinity sat reading a tiny book. Was that a New Testament Bible? "Sorry to interrupt."

She looked up and blinked rapidly. "It's fine. What's going on?"

He sucked in a breath. She looked like an angel curled up with the tiny Bible. He cleared his throat. "I have to leave, and I don't know when I'll be back. Protection Inc. will keep you safe." He wished he could stay, but duty called.

Her brow furrowed. "My location has been

compromised. Shouldn't I move?"

"No. Frank has retrofitted his home into a fortress over the past couple of months. With Carissa here, you'll be safe. The police will be on the lookout for trouble as well."

"What about the delivery man? Did anyone talk to him?"

He nodded. "A police officer questioned him."

"And?"

He glanced at his watch. "I'll tell you everything as soon as I'm able. Hang tight here. I'll be back tonight." At least he would if everything went according to plan.

"Okay. Be safe."

He hesitated when her gaze slammed into his. There was something in them that hadn't been there before. *Trust?* Wasn't it only a couple of days ago she was furious with him for not telling her about the tap on her phone? "You too." He turned and left, pushing aside thoughts of Trinity and their evolving relationship. His team needed him one hundred percent focused. They depended on him, and he would not let them down.

A short while later, he sat with Charlie, who was now in a suit and tie, along with Paige in the coffee shop a block away from the gallery. An undercover agent had gone ahead of them and secretly fed them a video feed of the goings on inside the gallery. Both Kendall and Alexis were there. Neither seemed alarmed or in a hurry to leave. Good. That would work to their advantage.

"What do you think?" Charlie asked. "They seem to be operating business as usual."

Paige nodded. "I don't get it. If Kendall is in on what's going down there, why hasn't she acted?"

He had given Kendall a lot of thought since reading that text. If he guessed correctly that Kendall was whom the informant referred to, then she had confidence he wasn't onto her, and she planned to play out her end game. "Arrogance. She believes she fooled me. So long as she knows what the FBI is doing she can work around us. For that matter she can play us. What she doesn't know is that we're onto her."

"Assuming you're correct," Paige said.

"Exactly." He had to be right. Kendall was literally the only person besides his team and those at Protection Inc. who knew about this operation. Protection Inc. only knew what they needed to know, which wasn't much.

Charlie pointed to the screen. "Look there."

Alexis and Kendall appeared to be having a tense conversation. Kendall gripped Alexis' arm. Her assistant pulled away and marched into the backroom.

"We need eyes back there," Charlie said to the tech guy listening to their conversation through their inner-ear communication devices. To anyone paying attention, they would assume they were talking on a phone.

"On it," the tech guy said from his van parked along the same street as the gallery. "I'm sending you the feed from their security cameras now."

The screen on Kyle's laptop flipped to the backroom of the gallery.

Charlie's phone rang. He looked at the caller ID. "It's about time. It's the gallery."

Kyle focused on Charlie, eager to hear this conversation.

"Mr. Sampson speaking," Charlie said.

"Put it on speaker," Kyle whispered.

Charlie pressed the speaker button.

"This is Alexis from Kendall Victoria Gallery. I have something I think you'll be interested in. I'm here all afternoon. When can you come by?"

Charlie looked at Kyle with a questioning gaze.

He held up one finger and mouthed one hour.

"My wife and I can be there in an hour."

"I have another interested buyer. I'll sell to the highest bidder."

"I see. Would you be able to send me a picture? It might not be to our liking. I hate to waste anyone's time."

"No. I'm sorry."

"We'll be there as soon as possible. You know Seattle traffic."

"Unfortunately," Alexis said in a pleasant tone. "See you soon."

Charlie ended the call. "That was weird. I thought she'd tell us a specific time. I think you have them rattled."

"Could be." If that were the case then maybe they'd

slip up and make things easier on all of them. Kyle pointed to the man in the backroom of the gallery with Alexis. "Do you think he's the other buyer?"

"Either that or the person who delivered it. He looks a lot like the man I saw enter the café. You said there's a connecting door between the two businesses?"

Kyle nodded. "You think he entered through the café to throw us off?"

"It's possible."

"Makes sense. The agent I sent to watch him said he was gone by the time he got there."

"I had eyes on the entrance the entire time. He didn't leave out the front."

"Then that man is likely the same one, and by the look of it, he brought the art."

"We need to detain him when he leaves." Charlie alerted plain clothes officers nearby to hold the man when he left the gallery.

Paige stood and hefted a duffle bag onto her shoulder. "I need to change into costume. Be back soon." She headed toward the restroom.

"You going to change too?" He asked Charlie.

"No. A suit and tie will suffice. How's Trinity doing?"

He raised a brow. "I'm surprised you care."

"She made my job harder than it needed to be but," Charlie shrugged, "I feel bad for her."

"She's strong."

"The bomb didn't freak her out?"

"I'm sure it did, but a lot has happened to her this week. She's held up like a pro."

"I noticed." Charlie frowned. "I hate admitting it, but I think I might have misjudged your friend. Since you've been involved with her, I decided to dig a little into her life and work. She's actually a pretty fair reporter. She gets her facts right too from what I listened to."

"It's hard to keep thinking of her as a bad guy when you see all the good she's done, huh?" He had to admit it too. Trinity, though flawed at times, was a genuinely good woman. Someone he could see himself with.

"Yeah. I suppose you're right," Charlie said begrudgingly.

"Aw, come on. She's pretty great. I've never met anyone like her." She was tough, strong, passionate, caring… He shook the thoughts away for now. When this operation ended, he planned to have a heart-to-heart with Trinity. He liked her and wanted to spend some time together when they weren't looking over their shoulders for bad guys.

"Not that it matters, but when this is all over, you have my blessing."

Kyle shifted his gaze off the screen and onto Charlie for a second. "Thanks."

"You should ask Trinity out. The two of you have a connection."

He had every intention of asking her out but was surprised by Charlie's observation.

"What?" Charlie shrugged. "We've been friends a long time. It's obvious you're interested in her."

"How do you figure?" To his way of thinking, he'd hid his feelings well, even from himself at times, but after the bomb this afternoon, there was no more pretending he didn't feel something more than compassion for Trinity. He admired her strength and work ethic among other things.

Paige, in her glammed-up disguise, dropped her duffel beside the table and sat. "What are we talking about?"

"Kyle dating Trinity."

"You're dating?" Surprise filled her voice.

"No."

"But he wants to." Charlie stood and buttoned his suit jacket at the waist. "Let's do this."

"Hey," Kyle said. "Remember, we need verbal proof that they're aware the art is stolen, or we don't have a case."

Charlie and Paige nodded and left.

Fencing stolen property was often hard to prosecute, and he needed this case to be solid. If he could prove Alexis was behind all of Trinity's trouble, all the better.

Kyle stayed put. He would watch all the players from here on his computer. FBI agents along with local authorities were strategically in place. If anyone spotted him near the gallery, it could tip off the players, and he couldn't have that.

Motion on the screen drew him from his thoughts. Alexis took a box from the man in the backroom and opened it.

Kyle leaned in closer to the screen. Was that *The Concert* by Johannes Vermeer? It had been missing since 1990. The piece was said to be one of the most valuable unrecovered stolen paintings ever. Last he'd read, the Baroque-style painting was valued at over $200,000,000.

It couldn't be the actual original though. It had to be a print—the FBI had tried for years to recover this piece to no avail. Now the statute of limitations had passed, but if they could prove they were trying to sell known stolen art, they could build a case and prosecute anyway.

He tapped the device in his ear and spoke. "They have *The Concert* in the backroom. I want eyes on it. Confirm it's the real deal."

Silence.

He looked back at the screen. Charlie and Paige walked into the gallery. Kendall greeted them and ushered them to the backroom.

"I want to hear what's going on in there."

A second later the conversation streamed into his earpiece.

Charlie shook Alexis' hand. "My wife and I are anxious to see what you have for us."

"This is an original Vermeer," Alexis said. "As I'm sure you know, a piece of this age has to be stored in a specific way to preserve it." She held it up and turned it around. "*The Concert* is in exceptional condition and will take top dollar."

Paige gasped. "That's the original?"

"That's correct," Kendall said. "Our seller on the east coast has been selling off his art through us for the past year. This is the last piece in his collection and the most valuable of them all."

Charlie reached his hand toward the painting, sealed behind glass. "It's superb." He looked from Alexis to Kendall. "You do know this was stolen?"

"I am aware," Kendall said. "But you don't need to worry. The statute of limitations has run out, so if it's ever discovered in your possession, you can't be prosecuted. Alexis assured me this would not be a problem for you." Her gaze shifted to the man standing nearby who'd remained silent.

"It's not," Charlie said quickly. "I just didn't expect a work of this stature and fame."

Alexis laughed. "Come now. Let's not play coy. I researched you, and we both know you dabble in stolen art."

Charlie raised a brow. "You surprise me. How much for the piece?"

Satisfaction shot through Kyle. The backstory they'd planted on the dark web about Charlie's alias had worked.

"Fifty million cash," Kendall said. "It's a bargain."

"What did your other buyer offer?" Charlie asked.

"He wasn't interested after all."

She was playing them. There was no other buyer, but why lie? It didn't work to her advantage for Charlie to believe the other buyer backed out when she could have lied and created a bidding war. Kyle couldn't figure out this woman. What was her game? At least now, he knew for certain she was the person Trinity's informant had been referring to.

"I'll need time to secure the cash," Charlie said.

"You have two hours." Kendall escorted him to the door leading to the gallery space.

Paige ran her fingers along Charlie's arm. "Sweetie, I think I'll wait here while you go to the bank. I want to look around and visit with our new friends."

"Of course, dear." Charlie left.

"Good job, Paige." Kyle said to himself softly. He made the necessary call to have the money ready for the operation while never taking his focus off the screen.

He had chosen a table that allowed him to sit with his back to a wall in a corner so no one could look over his shoulder or glance his way to see what he was looking at. He sipped his iced coffee, nursing it to last as long as possible. The shop had enough foot traffic that no one noticed him, but not so much that he was in the way.

Paige wandered around the gallery and stopped at a piece that looked similar to the one Kendall had once showed him.

Kendall stopped beside her. "Do you like it?"

"I do. It's different."

"I agree. It's not what I had expected from this artist, but there is something special about it. Should I add it to you purchase?"

"Mm. I think not. It's too pedestrian for our collection. Now if you had something that would complement our purchase, I would consider it."

"We're getting out of that side of the business. It's become too… risky."

Paige shrugged as if she didn't care either way. "I wish we would have stopped by sooner. My husband had a basement gallery constructed at our house, and we could use a few more special pieces."

"You must have an amazing collection."

"It's not bad."

"If you don't mind me asking, what do you plan to do with your purchase? Will it be in your personal gallery, or do you have another plan for the piece?"

Paige tsked and waved a finger in the air. "I cannot reveal such a thing to a seller of," she looked around and lowered her voice to a stage whisper, "stolen art. What's to stop you from taking it back and reselling it?"

"Touché." A strained smile touched Kendall's lips. "However, I can assure you I am not a thief. I'm simply a woman providing a service."

Charlie walked into the gallery holding a briefcase.

"That was fast." Kendall smiled. "Shall we?" She motioned to the backroom.

The three joined Alexis and the man who still stood silently in the background.

"I trust you have something for me to transport the piece in." Charlie placed the briefcase on a table and opened it.

Alexis stepped forward. "Of course. My associate," she motioned to the silent man, "will take care of that for you while I count the money."

Kyle sighed. It figures she would count it. Was the silent man the shooter from the Wharf? He tapped the device in his ear. "Find out who the associate is."

Paige stepped over to the man. "And who are you?"

The man didn't respond, acting as though he never heard the question.

Alexis moved close to Paige. "Gus is a silent partner. Let's give him some space. He doesn't like people to crowd him."

"Crowd him? As if." Paige stuck her nose up and strutted toward her *husband*. "Are we almost finished? I'm getting a headache."

Kyle sucked in a breath at the code phrase. "He's armed." He had figured someone would be armed, but the confirmation was helpful. Based on their formfitting clothing, he doubted the women were carrying weapons.

Kendall finally closed the briefcase. "It's all there. It's been a pleasure. Gus?"

Gus pulled his gun.

"Whoa." Charlie raised his hands. "What's going on?"

"You talk too much," Gus said. "Move."

"Go!" Kyle commanded. "Move in. There's one armed male along with two undercover agents and two other women in the backroom."

Within seconds, FBI agents and local law enforcement stormed the gallery.

Charlie kicked the gun from the man's hand, sending it flying across the room.

Paige twisted Kendall's arm behind her back.

Agents breached the backroom. "FBI!"

Kyle closed the laptop and raced up the block to the gallery. He entered the backroom of the gallery and immediately spotted Kendall and her cronies in handcuffs being escorted from the back. He raised a hand to stop their progress. "I have one question. Which one of you shot at us?"

Gus smirked.

"You're a lousy shot."

"Those were warning shots. If I wanted to kill you I would have."

Kendall looked at Kyle as if he were the criminal. "I thought you trusted me. Were you setting me up?"

"Not intentionally, but as soon as I realized my error, I acted."

She glared at him.

"There's one thing I still can't figure out. What was up with the codes?"

She rolled her eyes. "Our supplier was nervous about the drop. He provided the codes for us to follow the clues to the location of the final drop."

"But you lost the codes."

"I'm well aware. We had a plan B, but for a time, our supplier was ready to kill to get the codes back."

He shook his head. Such an odd bunch of criminals.

A police officer led Kendall away.

Kyle walked over to his team and clapped them each on the shoulder. "Great job. I'm sure we have a case. Even if, for some crazy reason, the prosecutor chooses not to charge them for selling stolen property, we can get them for numerous other offenses."

"Did I hear Gus admit to shooting at us on the Wharf?" Paige asked.

"Sounded like that to me." Kyle grinned. It would be hours before he could see Trinity, but he'd call her from the car and let her know they solved the case. He still needed to locate her informant. He tossed Charlie the keys to the SUV. "You drive. I need to make a call."

They settled into the rig and pulled away. Crime scene techs would process the scene. He pressed Trinity's number.

She answered on the first ring. "What's happening?"

"We got them. Here's your exclusive. You ready?"

"Mind if I record your statement?"

"Not at all."

"Okay. Ready."

"Art gallery owner, Kendall Victoria and her assistant Alexis McKenna, used the gallery to fence stolen art to wealthy customers. FBI agents recovered *The Concert* by Johannes Vermeer. The piece was stolen in 1990 from a gallery in Boston. I'll let you do your own research on the painting."

Trinity blew out a long breath. "Wow. I sure didn't expect such a famous piece. I'll let my boss know and work on a breaking news story. Thanks for the scoop."

"Sure thing." His heart skipped a beat at the thought of Trinity continuing to follow the story. "Stay safe, Trinity. This isn't over for you yet. We need to find the person behind the bomb. You're still not out of trouble."

# 17

Trinity looked into the camera as she broke the news live from Frank's backyard. Carissa had strongly recommended she do the shot from there, so the news station sent her a cameraman. "Acting on a tip last Sunday, I discovered an art smuggling ring, fencing stolen art out of the Kendall Victoria Gallery in Seattle. I gave the information to the FBI. Late this afternoon, the FBI recovered *The Concert* by Johannes Vermeer. The piece was stolen in 1990 from a gallery in Boston. Three people are in custody, including the owner of the business, Kendall Victoria and her assistant, Alexis McKenna. I'm Trinity Lockhart. Back to you at the station." She waited for the light to go off on the camera and then relaxed.

"Looked good," Tim, her new cameraman, said.

"Thanks. I guess I'll see you on Monday." Working with Tim brought to mind Rick. Her old cameraman would be greatly missed. Her stomach sickened thinking about how he died.

Tim nodded as he headed for the gate with the equipment. "See you soon." He waved before stepping through the gateway.

Carissa gave her a thumbs-and up and then motioned to Trinity to head inside from her position at the gate, which she locked up as soon as Tim cleared the yard.

Carissa met up with her in the living room where she sat with the evening news playing on the television. "How you doing?"

"I'd be much better if we knew who my informant was. Can't they trace the text messages I received?"

"I'm sure they tried, but if it was a burner phone, it wouldn't do them any good."

"Of course. When are you leaving?"

"Soon. Frank is across the street with Katrina. They'll bring dinner. Then I'll head out for the night."

Trinity nodded. She liked these people and wished they could be in her life all the time, though not as her protectors. They represented what she believed a family should be. They really cared for one another. Not that her dad didn't care for her, but he had issues, which made it difficult for her to feel safe, loved, and cared for.

"What are you thinking about?" Carissa closed and locked the sliding glass door.

"How I'm going to miss all of you when this is over."

"That's nice of you to say, but maybe we'll run into

one another from time to time."

Trinity couldn't imagine why that would happen but nodded to be polite.

The front door opened. "It's just us," Frank said. "Who's hungry? We have roasted chicken with roasted carrots and potatoes."

"Sounds like Katrina went all out," Carissa said.

Frank and Katrina walked into the kitchen each carrying a covered platter.

"Wish I could stay, Frank, but Marc is expecting me for dinner." Carissa sniffed the air. "It sure smells good, Katrina."

"Thanks. I'm sorry you have to leave."

Carissa shrugged into her coat. "I'll see you tomorrow, Trinity."

"Hold up," Frank said. "I received a call from Trinity's boss. The news station is no longer covering her protection."

Trinity gasped. "You're kidding." Though she didn't know why she was surprised when she'd been shocked that the station had picked up the tab to begin with.

"I wish. He said he got his story and to cut you loose."

"Wow. Guess I see where I rank." Although surprised the station had covered her protection detail, she didn't expect to be cut loose when her informant was still at large. "Is he aware my informant tried to kill me today?"

Frank nodded. "I told him, but it didn't change anything."

"That's nuts." Carissa's jaw thrust forward and her brow furrowed.

Trinity blew out a breath. "It's all good. Since my informant got what he wanted, maybe I'll be safe. Remember he was angry that Kyle had trusted Kendall."

Frank nodded slowly as if in thought. "True. There has to be a personal connection between your informant and the gallery."

"How so?" Carissa asked.

"Think about it. The text Trinity received was angry, and he felt betrayed. It was personal for him. He wanted to take them down, and he was angry when it looked like Trinity ruined the opportunity. I have to wonder why he cared that much. Why he was willing to kill when Trinity failed."

"I see where you're going with this." Carissa shot a concerned look at Trinity and then looked back at Frank. "If I come up with any ideas, I'll let you know. Gotta go now though." She waved to Katrina then left.

Trinity's stomach growled.

Katrina chuckled. "I was going to say I hope you're hungry."

"My stomach doesn't know how to keep a secret. Is there anything I can do to help?"

"Thanks but all I need to do is remove the covers."

"It smells delicious." Frank stood behind Katrina and wrapped his arms around her middle then placed a kiss on her neck.

Trinity chuckled. Frank was a different man when Katrina was in the room. "Maybe I should take my food up to the guestroom and hang out there until Kyle comes to get me."

"Don't you dare." Katrina playfully swatted a serving spoon at Frank. "Behave. You're making Trinity uncomfortable."

"Oh no, it's all good," Trinity said quickly. "I only thought you could use some alone time."

"The offer is appreciated, but not necessary." Frank took three plates from the cupboard. He bowed his head and closed his eyes. "Thank You, Lord, for the food and for the hands that prepared it. Bless it to our bodies. In Jesus name, amen." He handed Trinity a plate. "Or would you rather tell us what you want, and we dish it up?"

"That would be appreciated. I'm right-handed, and I don't want to make a mess." Though so far, she hadn't done too badly. "Your prayer reminded me of something I wanted to tell you."

"Oh yeah. What?"

Frank placed a piece of chicken on a plate and a spoonful of mixed, roasted veggies.

"Carissa gave me one of your New Testament Bibles earlier today. She said it was okay."

He placed the plate in front of her. "She was correct. Have you started reading it?"

"Only the passages Carissa marked."

"What did you think?"

She shrugged. "I need to read it again on a day when life isn't so distracting."

He nodded. "Good idea."

The couple filled their plates and joined her at the bar where it appeared to be the normal place to eat in this house.

Her mind wandered to Kyle. She wished he was here with her right now but appreciated how hard he'd worked to take down the art traffickers. She finished up the food on her plate. "Thank you for the delicious meal, Katrina, but now I hope you will both excuse me. It's been a day, and I need to decompress."

"You're welcome," Katrina said. "I probably won't see you again before you leave. Take care, Trinity."

"I will. You too." Trinity walked up the stairs to the guestroom. She pulled out the little New Testament and sat on the bed, her back propped against the headboard. Maybe this would ease the butterflies in her stomach. Something felt wrong, but other than the fact her informant was on the loose and she'd lost her protection, she couldn't place what it was.

Late Friday evening the doorbell rang. Trinity had joined Frank downstairs a short while ago since Kyle had yet to show, and she was getting sick of hanging out in the room alone.

"That's probably Kyle now." Frank stood and walked to the door.

Frank and Kyle talked softly in the other room.

Apparently, they didn't want to let her in on whatever it was they were discussing. Too bad. She stood. It was her life at stake, and if they were talking about her, she wanted to know.

"That's great news," Frank said.

Relief and happiness poured through her at the same time. She hadn't realized how much she'd missed him. "What's great news?" Trinity called out as she walked toward the front of the house.

Both men turned her direction.

"Well?" she asked. Her heart fluttered at the sight of Kyle even though the dark circles rimming his eyes made him look like he could sleep for a solid week. This man had grown on her in a way she hadn't expected. She'd miss him when he sent her packing.

"We have all the players in the smuggling ring in custody. Including Ashley, the niece of the café owner."

"You're kidding. How did you find out she was involved?"

Kyle ambled toward her. "Let's go sit."

She'd noticed the front room by the entrance was barren but hadn't thought to ask about it with so much going on. Frank ought to make it his dining room considering the number of people he entertained with no place to eat but the kitchen bar. "What's the deal with this empty room, Frank?"

"It's wasted space. I like hanging out in the back of the house."

She could attest to the truth of that and shrugged.

To each their own. "It'd make a good dining room. Just saying."

"Hmm. Interesting idea. I'll think about that."

She sank back onto the couch and waited on the men to get settled.

"We knew that the gallery owner was close friends with the owner of the café and suspected she could be in on it, especially after seeing a suspect enter the café and never leave, yet he was nowhere to be found. Once we were able to rule out the café owner, we looked at the niece. As it turns out she and Alexis are roommates and thick as thieves."

Trinity rolled her eyes. "Very punny."

Frank chuckled. "That was a good one."

Kyle grinned. "Anyway, Ashley was spotted entering the gallery from the secret door—she thought everyone was gone and went straight to a hidden safe in the floor beneath some boxes."

"Oh my goodness! That's crazy. She was going to steal the cash and run." Trinity shouldn't be surprised.

"Yes." Kyle reached for her hand. "It's not all good news though."

Her pulse picked up and her gaze shot to his. "Is this about my informant?"

He nodded. "The police are working the case because of the bomb. They're doing their best, but as of now, they don't have a solid lead."

Frank cleared his throat. "Trinity's boss terminated his contract with Protection Inc. for Trinity's security this evening."

Kyle sighed. "It figures he'd do that. He got what he wanted."

Trinity gave Kyle's hand a squeeze. "It's okay. I'll be fine. My informant wanted us to stop the art traffickers, and we did. I'm sure he'll leave me alone since he got what he was after."

Frank frowned. "Have either of you asked yourselves why he was so set on stopping the sale of stolen art?"

Trinity tilted her head to the side. "That's a good question. What does he have to gain by the smuggling ring being stopped?"

"Exactly." Frank stood and walked to the kitchen. He filled a glass with water from the tap. "Anyone else want water?"

"No, thanks," Kyle and Trinity said in unison.

"Could have been revenge." She had seen plenty of true-life crime stories motivated from revenge. "Maybe they double-crossed him or cut him out."

"I'll look into that. Tomorrow." Kyle stood. "I'm going back to my place. Since it's late, you're welcome to the basement, Trinity. Or at the very least, you can retrieve your car."

Her stomach did a flip. He was cutting her loose. Somehow, she'd expected him to stay by her side until the bomber was found and arrested. Her throat thickened and the backs of her eyes burned. She blinked and got a hold on her emotions. She didn't want to lose it in front of these men. Especially Kyle. "I'd appreciate a ride to my car. I'm looking forward to a night in my own bed."

"I thought you might be."

Frank's brow furrowed. "I don't like it. You really think the bomber's going to leave Trinity alone? He tried to annihilate her earlier today, and you're comfortable leaving her to her own devices?"

Kyle frowned. "What would you have me do, Frank?"

"Stick by her side. Watch her back."

"I never said I wasn't doing that. As it happens, the feds are interested in this bomber. Trinity isn't going to be able to go anywhere without a tail."

Her eyes widened. "For real? Why didn't you say so?"

"It's been a long day, and it slipped my mind. You really thought I'd be so cavalier with your life?" He almost looked perturbed.

"Not really, but I…" She shrugged and pressed her lips together. Kyle was in a mood. Sometimes, silence was best. Besides, she really had thought he was letting her loose. He was under no obligation to her, though she'd hoped he would stick by her.

"Then let's get you to your car so you can do something about that."

"Sounds great." She started to walk to the door then pulled up short. "I can't drive with a broken arm."

"Your car is a stick?" Frank asked, his tone indicating his surprise.

"It was cheaper than an automatic. It's not ideal in hilly Seattle, but it's not that big of a deal."

Respect shone in Kyle's tired eyes. "I'll take you home. Tomorrow we can get you a rental until your cast is removed."

"I can take the bus. The Park and Ride isn't far from my apartment."

"No. Public transportation is out of the question right now." Kyle clapped Frank on the shoulder. "Thanks for everything."

"I'm only a phone call away if you need anything."

"I know, and I appreciate that." Kyle turned toward Trinity. "You ready?"

She nodded, noting her neck felt much less stiff and sore than it had. At least one thing was going right. How was she supposed to sleep, knowing someone wanted her dead? Sure, she talked brave to the men, but seriously, someone tried to kill her today, and she was supposed to forget it happened and go on with life as normal. Nope. Even she couldn't do that. She wouldn't rest until her informant was found.

# 18

Trinity gazed toward the water as she sat on her covered patio breathing in the night air. The sliding glass door opened. Trinity jumped and whirled around. "Kyle." She held a hand to her chest. "I thought you left."

He stood holding two mugs. "I'm sorry for scaring you. I was in the process of heading out when I spotted herbal tea bags on the counter and thought you might enjoy some."

She grinned. "Thank you." She reached up and took the mug he offered. "Have a seat. I love sitting out here on clear nights." A hush hovered in the night air. You could hear a pin drop it was so quiet out here tonight. No one would be able to sneak up on them without giving themselves away.

He eased into the basic plastic patio chair she'd found at a garage sale last summer. "It is nice out here. I can see why you enjoy it."

"Yeah. It's my favorite way to relax at the end of a

long day." She sipped the lavender tea. "I've been doing nothing but thinking this evening."

He shifted to better face her. "What about?"

"My informant and the people you arrested. I really think they're connected in some way. Perhaps he's a scorned lover or a former employee."

Kyle nodded. "I've wondered the same. I plan to follow the idea tomorrow." He sipped the tea and made a face.

"Not a fan of lavender?"

"I guess not." He set the mug on the ground beside him.

"Don't you have tomorrow off since it's Saturday?"

"I do, but it won't stop me from digging into the lives of Ashley, Alexis, and Kendall. The sooner we find the bomber, the sooner you'll be safe."

"I like the sound of that." She especially appreciated that he cared enough to go the extra mile for her. "If there's anything I can do, please let me know."

"Do you have plans for this weekend?"

"Other than hanging out here, no. Though I wish I did." With a broken arm and no way to get around except public transportation, she planned to stay put here until Monday.

"I might be able to help with that. Thought we could have dinner together tomorrow."

Her breath caught. Was he saying what she thought? "As in a date, or does it have to do with the bomber?"

"A date." He dipped his head to the side.

"I'd like that very much. Can we go to Cactus in Bellevue Square? I love that place. They have the best Mexican food."

"Sounds good." He stood. "Okay, I have to come clean. I had no intention of leaving you alone and not protected tonight. I was hoping you'd stay at my apartment, but I didn't want to pressure you. Do you mind if I crash on your couch?"

This man was full of surprises. "I'd like that very much." She stood. "I'll go grab some linens for you." She went inside, placed the mug on the kitchen counter and then pulled open the linen closet door.

"I've got it."

Kyle's breath warmed her neck. A shiver ran through her. She stepped aside. "Sleep well." She hesitated for a second. "Thank you for everything, Kyle. It's been a challenging week for both of us, and I know I'm the cause."

"'Cause you're a troublemaker," he teased. He faced her and reached for her hand.

A tingle zipped up her arm. Her gaze locked on his.

"I'm thankful you trusted me and came to me when you needed help." He moved toward her slowly. Close enough that he had to tilt his head to keep from bumping noses.

He was going to kiss her! She closed her eyes and leaned in.

A soft kiss pressed against her forehead. "Sleep well."

Her eyes popped open. "You too." Her face heated. She went into her room and closed the door. Her heart beat a rapid staccato. She held her cool hand to her overly warm checks as she leaned against the door. She'd thought for sure he was going to give her a real kiss. How embarrassing. Hopefully, he hadn't noticed her lean in.

Had she read him wrong, or had he changed his mind? Why would he change his mind? Maybe the bomber still at large had something to do with it. What about their dinner date? Her laptop sat on the dresser. She took it to her bed. She could sleep all day tomorrow. Tonight, she was going to cyber stalk the people arrested at the gallery.

Kyle stared up at Trinity's apartment ceiling from his position on the couch, calling himself a coward. No. He wasn't a coward, only cautious. Until that bomber was behind bars and Trinity's life wasn't on the line, he would keep things between them professional or at least as close to professional as one could be after expressing himself the way he had and asking her on a dinner date. He stifled a groan, sat up and punched the hard pillow in a shape that better suited him, and rested back down.

His phone buzzed. He reached for it and read the text message.

*Well done FBI. But it's too late for your girlfriend.*

He surged upright. *How'd you get this number?*

*Wrong question.*

He quickly placed a call to see if the text messages could be traced.

*You're running out of time.*

*Who are you? How did you know about the gallery?*

*That's more like it. I met your girlfriend once. Twice actually. But Kendall knows me very well.*

*What's going to happen to Trinity?* He stared at his phone. Nothing. He put the phone to his ear. "Did you get it?"

"He's currently at a gas station on Bellevue Way. From your location, it will be the first one you come to."

"Got it." He thrust his feet into his shoes and raced out the door, locking it behind him. "Send local police to that location. I need the person using that phone. Consider him armed and dangerous." He ran to his vehicle and tore out of the parking lot. Five minutes later, he pulled into the gas station. Good, the police were already there. He got out and approached the one nearest to him. "I'm FBI Special Agent Richards. I called this in. Did you locate the person with the phone?"

The officer frowned. "Negative. We found the gas attendant, a young man with the phone, but he swears he's not your guy. Said some dude in his thirties gave it to him and tore out of here in an older model BMW."

"I'll need to see their surveillance video."

"Good luck without a warrant."

"The man who gave him that phone sent a bomb to

a friend of mine today."

"I heard about that. Happened in Seattle, right?"

"Yes. Excuse me." He strode over to the gas attendant. Showed his badge and explained the situation. "I'd like to see your surveillance footage. It's the only lead we have on the bomber."

The young man's eyes grew wide. "Bomber? He looked so normal." He pressed some keys on a keyboard and pulled up the time the man had been inside. "There."

"Can you pause it?"

The screen paused.

He snapped a pic with his phone. "Keep playing."

The young man pressed a key and the video continued. "He doesn't look at the camera."

"I noticed. Thanks for your help. I'll have the officers get a warrant for a copy of this." He walked over to the officers and filled them in on what he needed. "Thanks. I need to go." He handed them his business card. "Please let me know when you have the copy." He left and headed back to Trinity's apartment.

He pulled up, parked, and then headed to her door. It was open! He pulled his sidearm and went inside. Everything looked as it had when he'd left. He went to Trinity's room. The door was open and she was gone. Everything looked as it should, minus Trinity. He sucked in a breath and called 9-1-1.

Trinity struggled against the restraints that wrapped her

good arm and the center of her body to a wooden chair in the backroom of the art gallery.

"Why are we here?" She asked her abductor who looked so familiar she was almost certain they'd met. Could he be the man who had bumped into her at the gallery that night?

"You are the grand finale. If you'd done what I asked, none of this would be happening."

"But I did. You said go to the exhibit. I went. I discovered two people back here, one wielding a gun."

"I saw you, but you went to the FBI. The job was for you. Not them."

"I don't understand. Didn't you want them stopped and arrested?"

"I wanted Kendall humiliated, like she humiliated me."

"I'm sure she is humiliated." Her search of Kendall online had showed multiple relationships with various men. "Did you date her once?"

"Worse than that. I proposed. In a very public way, and she turned me down in front of thousands of people. I became a gif." He looked away. "She laughed in my face and told me she had been dating two other men. I thought we were exclusive."

"I'm sorry. No one deserves that kind of humiliation. That had to hurt." In spite of everything she kind of felt bad for the man, but at the same time, she wanted to knock his lights out for putting her through this.

"You have no idea." He shook his head. "If only you would have done a story on the gallery like I wanted. She would have been so embarrassed she might have even closed her precious business."

"I did do the story!" Anger surged through Trinity. "What are you whining about? The gallery *is* closed. Kendall is in custody. On top of that, because of the piece the FBI found her with, the story went national. The entire nation knows what Kendall Victoria did. Even if charges don't stick, her life in the art world is over."

"You don't get to talk to me like that!" Spittle spewed from his mouth, and he yanked out a gun. "I wanted it all on camera! I wanted you to confront her and humiliate her on live TV. All you did was show her picture. Big whoop. She's behind bars and safe from the outside world and her critics. All that work I went to. I followed her every move. Listened in on her phone conversations. Fed you information all for nothing. You ruined everything."

Trinity's heart pounded. She was done for. This was the end. *Why, Lord, did You give me such a rotten life? You're supposed to love me. I'm supposed to be able to trust You.*

*Trust Me.*

Overwhelmed, she fought tears as something unexplainable settled over her. *I'm supposed to just trust You after You let him get me?*

*I'm here. Trust Me.*

She had nothing to lose. *Okay. I trust You.* The fear vanished. Her gaze returned to her abductor who paced back and forth near the garage door in the backroom of the gallery. "Now what?"

"Now I burn this place to the ground." He walked to a corner and picked up a red gasoline can.

She swallowed the lump in her throat. "Someone lives upstairs. You'll have two lives on your hands, and she didn't do anything to you."

"What difference does it make? So long as you suffer, I don't care. I'm so sick of women burning me."

Clearly, this dude was damaged. But she could not allow him to take it out on her. She looked around the room for some way to get free. "You never told me your name." She had to keep him talking. The longer he talked the better chance she had of making it out of this alive. She spotted a fire extinguisher with a fire alarm pull on the wall a few feet from where she sat. If she could slide over to it, she could take her arm from the sling, pull the alarm, and then spray him with the extinguisher. It would hurt like crazy, and she wasn't even sure her fingers would be able to pull the alarm, but she had to try.

"Todd."

"What's your last name?" She scooted an inch toward the alarm.

"Just Todd." He picked up the can and splashed the fuel around the room.

She slid a little closer and almost tipped.

"Hey! What are you doing?" His gaze landed on the alarm. "You've got guts, lady, but it's too late. I hope you're ready to meet your maker."

Trinity closed her eyes. *God, I trust You. When I open my eyes, I'll either be in heaven or You'll have intervened. I'm okay either way, but I would like to live.*

# 19

Kyle sped across the 520 toward Seattle. He'd received a call that the surveillance on the gallery had caught activity inside. A man and a woman were spotted entering from the alley.

Normally, the local police would beat him there, but a fatal crash on I-90 and then an apartment fire a few blocks from the gallery, among other incidents, had everyone spread thin. He looked up—a full moon. Full moons seemed to bring trouble every time. Thankfully, 1:00 AM traffic was light.

He slammed on his brakes when a car cut him off. "Seriously?" He changed lanes and sped past the clueless driver. He hoped and prayed Trinity was the woman seen going into the gallery. He exited the bridge and took the quickest route to the gallery. He slowed and stopped in the same spot he and Trinity had parked on Monday.

He checked his weapon and got out being careful to close the door with a quiet click. One car sat parked in the alley facing out. The driver wanted a fast exit. He jogged across the street. The garage door was open. He poked his head around the corner and spotted Trinity tied to a chair.

Her abductor splashed fuel around the room. "This is going to destroy Kendall." He laughed. "Can you imagine the look on her face when she finds out everything she worked for has gone up in flames?"

"You're probably doing her a favor. I'm sure she has insurance," Trinity said.

How was she so calm?

The man stilled, and a series of expletives spewed from his mouth. "No more talking." He pulled a matchbook from his pocket and then walked toward the garage door.

This was it. Kyle counted down in his mind three, two, one, and then leapt onto the man taking him to the ground landing on top of him. Air rushed from his lungs. He was stunned only a second and sucked in a breath before the man beneath him could fight back. Kyle slapped a cuff on one wrist then pulled the other to meet it. "You okay, Trinity?"

"I am now. Where are the police?"

"Tied up. Kind of like you." He grinned and chuckled when she rolled her eyes. Relief coursed through him. This was finally over.

Dillon stepped through the garage door opening. "I heard you needed an assist." He hustled over to Trinity, pulled out a knife, and cut the ropes trapping her.

"Sorry I'm a little late to the party."

"Better late than never." Kyle helped his prisoner stand. "You able to run him in?"

"I need to secure the scene first." He walked out of the building.

Kyle stood in the alley, holding his prisoner. "We'll wait. How is it you're on duty tonight? I thought you worked the day shift."

"Shift change. Personally, I don't really mind, but tonight has been crazy. Not the way I like to start a new schedule." He pulled crime scene tape from the trunk of his squad car, which blocked the driveway. "Backup is on the way. Should be here in under five minutes."

Trinity finally stood. Uncertainty rested on her face.

Kyle tilted his head toward the car. "My car is parked in the same place as before. You can wait inside for me."

"No, thanks. I'd rather stick with you." Her voice shook slightly. "His name is Todd. Just Todd." She glared at the man.

"Let's go, Todd." Kyle guided him to the police cruiser. He removed a knife and a pistol from his prisoner as he patted him down and then put him into the backseat. He stood outside the car, unwilling to leave the man alone for even a second.

Trinity stood along the exterior of the garage door near where Dillon worked. "If you close the garage won't the fumes from the gasoline build up?"

Dillon frowned. "I won't close the door. This needs

to be cleaned up." Using his radio he called in about the gasoline. "I hadn't noticed the smell until you mentioned it. I worked at a gas station right out of high school and grew accustomed to the smell."

Trinity nodded and stayed planted between him and Dillon, seemingly unwilling to get too close to the squad car even though she clearly didn't have an issue with Dillon. Perhaps because he'd stepped in to help out with her protection at the hospital.

Two more squad cars pulled to a stop and officers emerged on the scene. Kyle showed his badge and briefly filled them in. He and Trinity would give statements at the station. He'd take her for a coffee first though. She looked ready to drop.

Dillon approached and spoke with the two officers then turned to Kyle. "I need to get your statement."

"We'll meet you at the precinct in an hour?"

"Make it thirty minutes."

Kyle nodded once. "See you soon." He held out a hand to Trinity who had followed Dillon over to the car. Her freezing fingers grasped his hand. "Let's get you warmed up. I know a twenty-four-hour coffee shop on the way to the precinct."

"Sounds good to me." She clutched his hand tightly as they walked to his car. He opened the passenger door for her and settled her inside. Then he retrieved a blanket from his trunk.

Dillon pulled away from the scene and waved as he passed.

Kyle waved back and got behind the wheel. He settled the blanket over Trinity then headed for the coffee shop. "You doing okay?"

"I don't know. I feel so many things right now. Gratitude that I'm alive. Anger. Relief. Remorse."

"Remorse?"

"Seeing the depravity of humanity makes me sad. I try to not get emotionally involved with the stories I do, but Todd's anger took on a life of its own. It's like he lost his mind."

"You think he's crazy?" He didn't like the idea of the man pleading insanity.

"No. Not insane, but he let his hurt and rage consume him so he acted in a way that was out of character. He might have an underlying mental health issue, but I'm not a doctor, just an observer."

Kyle pulled into a parking spot at the coffee shop. "Want to come in or stay here?"

"I'm coming. Seattle at night is not my favorite place to be alone." She got out and met him at the hood.

They ordered two coffees then sat at a wooden table for four in the cozy shop. Kyle studied Trinity.

"You're going to give me a complex if you keep looking at me like you're afraid I'll break." Trinity sipped her coffee. "This is good."

He dipped his chin. "Yeah. Sorry for staring. Guess I'm trying to make sure you're okay. You went through a lot tonight."

She held up her left arm revealing a rope burn. "He didn't hurt me, other than a few bruises when he grabbed me from my room and then tied me up."

He winced. "We can get some ointment to help with that. Mind if I ask how he was able to get you so easily? Your room didn't look like you put up a fight."

She blew out a breath. "I was on my computer working. I get pretty intense, and I'm good at blocking out things going on around me. I felt safe because I knew... or rather thought... you were in the other room, and I didn't notice him until he tossed a lasso over my head and essentially hogtied me."

His mouth opened. Not much surprised him. "You're kidding."

"Nope. I was so surprised by him and his lasso I kind of froze." She shook her head. "I'm embarrassed. I should have fought back."

He agreed, but it probably wouldn't have done any good considering she had an arm in a sling from the accident earlier in the week. She likely would have injured herself worse. "It all worked out in the end."

"How did you know where to find me?"

"I didn't know for sure, but when activity was reported at the gallery I had a hunch."

She frowned and looked down at the cup she held. "Where did you go tonight? I was shocked that you were gone when he carried me from my bedroom."

He explained what had transpired. "He played me. Lured me into leaving the apartment so he could get to you. I'm sorry. I should have considered that he would circle back to your apartment." He would have to work hard to forgive himself for that.

Her gaze locked onto his. "I still trust you."

His eyes widened. "Thank you. You're different. What's changed?"

"Coming within minutes of being burned alive gives you a different perspective on life. Plus, I think God spoke to me tonight."

"Really? What'd He say?"

"Trust Me."

"And did you?"

"It's so weird. As soon as I gave in and decided to trust Him, I felt different. I wouldn't exactly say peaceful, but I was. It was overwhelming emotionally. I think now with a little distance from it, it was love. His love was overwhelming. I knew that no matter what happened, I was going to be okay. Even if okay meant I woke up in heaven."

Kyle's throat thickened. He blinked and cleared his throat. "I'm speechless."

She dabbed the corner of her eyes with a napkin. "I get that. Shouldn't we be going?"

"Yeah. Let's get this over with."

"You know what I can't wait for?" She looked at him with sparkling eyes.

"What's that?"

"That chicken enchilada you're buying me for dinner tonight. I'm ready to celebrate."

Trinity looked in the mirror one last time. She wore a teal color wrap dress with wedge boots and a denim jacket. She reached up, smoothed her straight hair, and then applied lip gloss. She dropped the gloss into her brown boho purse and headed for the living room.

She'd slept most of the day after Kyle brought her home with the promise of returning at five. He would be here any minute. Good thing too. She was starving. There would be no eating before their date so she could appear to not be a healthy eater. He already knew otherwise and besides, who needed that kind of pressure to be perfect—at least with him? She was still working on that concept with regard to the rest of the world.

A rap on the door made her smile. The man was punctual. After a quick glance through the peephole to confirm it was Kyle, she squared her shoulders and then pulled the door open.

Kyle stood with a bouquet of daisies. "For you."

How did he know she loved daisies? "Thanks. I love daisies. Come in while I put them in water."

He followed her inside. "You look pretty."

She filled a tall glass cup with water and looked over her shoulder. "And you look handsome. Of course you always do. I like this relaxed look on you." He wore chinos and a black button up shirt with a casual sports coat. "I assume the coat means you're armed."

"Always. You ready?"

She nodded, and they walked out together. "Did you get to sleep today?"

"For a few hours. I must admit I'm glad to have that operation behind me."

She locked up and walked with him to his car. "Do all your operations wrap up within a week?"

"No." He left it at that.

"I'm really looking forward to tonight."

"Me too, but there's something you should know before we get there."

"Uh-oh. That doesn't sound good."

"It depends on how you look at it. I might have mentioned to Marc that we were going to Cactus at Bellevue Square. He suggested we double date. I agreed since you and Carissa hit it off. Well, one thing led to another and the entire team is going to be there."

She groaned. "How did that happen?"

"Frank found out and wanted to bring Katrina. Then none of us wanted to leave out Sally."

"Poor Sally. She needs a date too."

"I have that covered. I figured at this point the more the merrier and made a reservation for nine."

"Nine? Who didn't you tell me about?"

"Charlie and Paige"

"What about Dillon?"

"He works."

"Right." Disappointment settled over her. She tried to shake it. These people had watched over her this week. They all deserved a celebratory dinner for a job well done. "Do I get a rain check for a night out with just the two of us?"

He glanced her way. "Absolutely. In fact I was thinking we could try going on the Big Wheel again."

"Umm. Too soon. How about the botanical garden here in Bellevue or the zoo in Seattle?"

"They both sound like fun. Let's wing it."

"Works for me."

Kyle found a parking spot, and they walked up the stairs to the second story restaurant. He opened the door for her. "There's Frank and Katrina."

"Hold the door." Marc reached out and grasped it above Kyle's hand. "I hear our double date turned into a party."

They all walked inside together.

Carissa spoke softly into her ear. "I'm glad you're okay. Marc filled me in on what went down this morning."

"It was intense, but I'm okay." Or at least she would be after a few counseling sessions that her boss insisted she have when he learned about the incident this morning. Before she collapsed in bed, she filed a story online as a follow-up to the arrests she reported on Friday night. She'd received a call within minutes from Clancy. He was concerned for her and wanted to check in to make sure she was safe. Guess he wasn't so bad after all.

Soon the table was filled with rambunctious laughter. Sally sat on her right and Kyle sat to her left.

Frank and Katrina were near Sally, and Carissa was directly across from her with Marc beside her. Then the FBI agents filled in the remaining seats. Paige and Charlie seemed to have warmed up to her.

Paige caught her attention. "Contrary to what this dude says, you're not so bad for a reporter." She bumped Charlie's shoulder.

Trinity raised a brow. "Still haven't forgiven me for the Sander's case? You know that wasn't my fault."

Charlie's face actually pinked. He hid behind a large glass of soda for a second. "Yeah whatever. You might be right. I might have misjudged you. I'm glad you're okay."

Trinity sat a bit taller. "That means a lot. Thanks. Both of you."

Kyle ducked his head, presumably to hide the huge grin on his face.

She nudged him in the ribs.

His shoulders shook. She joined in his laughter, and seconds later, their half of the table couldn't stop laughing. It felt good to relieve the stress of the week with laughter.

Two lessons she'd learned this week were that love was shown in many ways and that there were different kinds of love. Though she hadn't felt loved before, she did now. She looked around the large table the nine of them occupied and couldn't help feeling the love in this group of men and women who cared enough to put their lives on the line for others.

"How you doing?" Kyle spoke softly beside her. "You ready to get out of here?"

"As much fun as this has been, we probably should go. I see a line of people waiting for tables."

Kyle stood. "It's been fun catching up with all of you, but Trinity and I are going to take off." He handed Frank enough cash to cover their meals and tip. "Thanks for your help this week. I won't forget it."

Trinity stood beside Kyle. "That goes for me too. What you and your team do is…" Her throat thickened. She cleared it. "Thank you."

Frank nodded. "It's our pleasure. You take care."

She waved to everyone at the table and then left with Kyle. "That was the most fun I've had since possibly ever."

"Yeah? Me too." He draped an arm across her shoulder. "You up for dessert. I know a place that has amazing cheesecake. We can get a couple pieces to go and enjoy them out on your balcony."

"I like the sound of that."

Hand in hand, they went inside the mall and over to the Cheesecake Factory. She ordered a strawberry cheesecake, and he ordered an original. Less than an hour later they sat on her balcony, enjoying dessert.

She savored the last bite. "Oh my goodness, this was amazing."

Kyle touched the side of her mouth and rubbed. "You had a little strawberry sauce."

She was tempted to *accidentally* get some on the

other side. Maybe he would kiss that side clean. "Thanks."

His gaze focused on her lips.

Her breath caught. She would not let him get away with a forehead kiss again. She reached out and grabbed the lapel of his jacket and pulled him close and planted a kiss on his soft lips.

His warm lips responded with all the passion she'd been feeling.

She tilted her head back. "Now that's what I call finishing with a bang."

He chuckled and tapped her nose with his. "I should go."

She stood and walked with him to the door. "Good night."

He cradled her cheek with the palm of his hand. "Don't forget to let me know when you want to visit that church in person. I want to go too. I wouldn't want you to stumble into trouble. I mean after all you are a troublemaker."

She laughed at his teasing. This felt so nice. "How's tomorrow sound?"

He nodded. "Sounds perfect."

The End.

# Author Note

I hope you enjoyed reading *Dark Threat*! I always do research for my books, but this one was a little unique. To help me get into the head of my characters I watched YouTube videos of a couple female television news reporters. One of them filmed a day in the life and the other was a series. She showed her life at the station as well as at home. I learned a lot.

A friend of mine is an artist and has a gallery, so I picked her brain regarding the art aspect of the story. As usual I used my uncle, a retired cop, as a resource for my law enforcement questions.

The stolen piece named at the end of the book is an actual painting. I found the story behind the theft and history of the investigation to be fascinating. Other than the fact that it's a real painting, the rest was made up in my mind.

The final book in the series, *Personal Threat*, will release in September. It will feature Sally and Dillon during Christmastime. It's a short novella that I hope you will feel wraps up the series well.

If you enjoyed this book, I hope you will take the time to write a short review on Amazon or any other book site you use. Thanks in advance!

If you want to learn more about me or my books please check out my website kimberlyrjohnson.com

In conclusion, the publication of a book took a small village. I want to extend special thanks to Angela Strong for her excellent critique and Fay Lamb for her astute editing skills. This book wouldn't be what it is without the eagle eyes of my proofreaders and beta readers. Special thanks to all of you! I appreciate each and every one of you!

I also want to extend special thanks to those of you who continue to hold me up in prayer. Your messages to let me know you're praying for me mean so much! Getting the final two books of this series ready to publish during a pandemic has been a challenge. One would think it would be easier, but for this introverted woman who loves to write in complete silence, having my family home—one attending university online for much of the writing of this book and another working from home, presented challenges. My son is back at school now, and I'm starting to find my footing. I was even able to write the final book in this series. Yay!

Thank you so much for taking this journey with me. I loved writing this series!

Blessings,
Kimberly Rose Johnson

# More Books by Kimberly Rose Johnson

### Protection Inc.
*Direct Threat*
*Imminent Threat*
*Certain Threat*
*Dark Threat*
*Personal Threat* (September 2021)

### Law Enforcement Heroes
*Edge of Truth*

### The Librarian Sleuth
*The Sleuth's Miscalculation*
*The Sleuth's Dilemma*
*The Sleuth's Conundrum*
*The Sleuth's Surprise*

### Brides of Seattle
*Until I Met You*
*The Reluctant Groom*
*Simply Smitten*

## Melodies of Love

*A Love Song for Kayla*
*An Encore for Estelle*
*A Waltz for Amber*

## Sunriver Dreams

*A Love to Treasure*
*A Christmas Homecoming*
*Designing Love*

## Wildflower B&B Romance Series

*Island Refuge*
*Island Dreams*
*Island Christmas*
*Island Hope*

## Contemporary Novellas

*Brewed with Love*
*Sara's Gift*